D1598478

Island Concierge

A Kelly Palmer Cozy Mystery

Biggi Van Wormer

Chapter One

Kelly was woken up by a ray of sun shining on her face through an opening in the heavy curtains. She had a raging headache and could barely move her head. She could however recognize that she was lying in a strange hotel room and hear that someone was lying next to her, snoring gently and rhythmically. Then she realized shocked that she was naked. First, she just moved her pupils back and forth, trying to be very quiet, then she lifted her head slightly and saw that the person lying next to her was Charles, her boss. She stopped breathing. Her eyes were as big as saucers. A thousand thoughts rushed through her head as she got up as quietly and quickly as possible, grabbed her clothes and snuck toward the door of the suite. She had only had two or three drinks last night. Were they that strong? Had she had sex? She wasn't even on the pill since she didn't have a boyfriend. Should she get the morning after pill? How was she ever going to face Charles again?

She quickly slipped into her clothes, looked for her

purse, opened and closed the hotel room's door as quietly as possible. Did she have time to go home, shower and change? Yes, it was seven a.m. She'd be able to go home and be back by nine. She cursed that she had to do the "walk of shame" through the hotel to take the boat shuttle and was going to have to face the captain and his crew. Couldn't she work at a "normal" hotel that wasn't on an exclusive island where you needed a boat to get back and forth?

As Kelly snuck out the back door of the side wing, trying not to attract any attention, she realized she needed her sunglasses. The sun was already so bright that it blinded her. As she walked along the sparkling pool toward the main building, fishing for her sunglasses in her purse, she almost tripped over - a body. She screamed and took another look. It was Samantha, one of the two women belonging to the group that had arrived yesterday. The one that had been accused of pushing her coworker into the pool. She was as dead as a doornail. Two pool boys and Mary, an employee who was setting the tables on the back patio for breakfast, quickly walked up, alarmed by Kelly's screaming. Kelly looked up at the balconies. Samantha must have fallen off her balcony on the second or third floor – or she'd been pushed.

2

Chapter Two

Flashback / The day before:

A strong gusty wind came up, blowing napkins off some oceanfront tables on a patio next to an upscale pool bar. Palm trees swayed in the wind, their fronds blowing to the side like hula dancers stretching out their arms. The ocean, white foam on the gusty waves, turned as gray as the sky. A sudden deafening crack of thunder echoed through the sky, followed by a flash of lightning, making the bar guests jump out of their seats. Everyone ran for cover when the rain started, a heavy tropical downpour with giant drops, soaking everything and everyone from head to toe within seconds. A waiter ran after some airborne dollar bills fluttering toward the beach, oblivious to the rain.

Kelly Palmer, the Casa Bella's concierge, was having a meeting with her boss Charles Watson, the hotel's general manager. A group of businessmen and women was arriving today, and they were going through a checklist of activities Kelly had arranged for them. It was obvious that Charles was flirting with

Kelly. She had a crush on her tall handsome boss with the chiseled chin, thick brown hair and piercing blue eyes, but she tried to remain professional. Right now, their only concern was getting their laptops and themselves to safety. They found shelter under the thatched roof of the pool bar where an employee quickly handed them some pool towels. Drying off their laptops, arms, and faces, they huddled close to the bar with the other guests. It was almost a moot point because everyone was soaked already, but the thunderstorm was lingering right above them, and it was advisable to stay under cover. Loud claps of thunder and flashes of lightning unloaded around them as the downpour continued.

"Why don't we go behind the bar. It's so crowded here," proposed Charles. Scott, the bartender, heard him and lifted the hinged part of the bar to allow Charles and Kelly in. It was cramped, a bit awkward and too close for Kelly's comfort.

His arm brushed against hers and gave her the feeling of butterflies in her stomach she'd been getting for quite a while now when she was around him or even just thought of him. She stepped back, almost tripping over some bar supplies that fell over with a loud bang, almost louder than the thunder. She was about to fall backward. Charles reached out, held her arm and steadied her. For a beat, the entire bar was silent. Everyone seemed to be staring at her. Kelly felt her face turn beet red. The bartender as well as Charles were about to say something when the rain stopped as suddenly as it had begun. The sun came out, and a beautiful rainbow appeared across the sky on the horizon.

Everyone was distracted from Kelly's blunder and continued cleaning up and taking care of business. Kelly exhaled with a sigh of relief.

Most guests skittered to their rooms to change into dry clothes. Some didn't care and stayed to finish their meals or drinks, drying in the sun. Some still had to take care of their checks. Kelly exhaled and was glad to see that Charles wasn't making a big deal out of her clumsiness. He was already giving the bartender Scott - a sympathetic, dark blonde, young guy from New Orleans with a southern accent - some instructions.

"Make sure you only have your best staff on during the next few days. You know how important this group is for the resort and how challenging they were last time."

"Yes, sir," he replied with his southern drawl. "I remember them very well." Scott winked at Kelly who smiled back at him. She knew Scott could handle them.

Thunderstorms in the Keys were always dramatic, but they came and went in a heartbeat, and the humidity that had been unbearable before the storm was gone now. Charles glanced at the wet tables around the bar that the waiters were currently drying off.

"Well, it looks like we'd better continue our meeting in my office. Are you okay, or do you have to go and change?" He looked down and pointed at

Kelly's slightly wet skirt that was now clinging to her legs.

Kelly felt how she was about to blush again and looked down at her wet skirt, but it was made of a thin quick-drying fabric and didn't feel too bad.

She shook her head. "I'm fine. The guests are coming soon, and I need to go and talk to Max in the kitchen as soon as we're done."

"Okay, let's go." Charles started walking away from the ocean toward the old hotel that looked more like a big mansion, Kelly grabbed her laptop and hurried to catch up with him.

The three-story Bahamian-style building was characterized by wraparound verandas, shuttered doors, and windows. It was entirely white and looked very elegant. The surrounding tall palm trees, plumerias, ginger and other exotic plants gave it a tropical feel, even more so, some squawking yellow-naped amazons and other local birds in the trees. As they quickly walked past a water fountain and up a set of stairs onto a veranda filled with plantation furniture, some chickens scurried away. Charles nodded at a couple sitting in rocking chairs, having their afternoon tea, and continued inside the lobby where he passed the front desk and walked down a hallway on creaky old hardwood floors leading to his office. Kelly had a hard time keeping up with him in her pumps but followed him closely. She closed the office door and sat down in front of his desk, opening her laptop.

"Okay, what else do we have here?"

"Well, first we have the banquet tonight," she replied.

"So, Max is working the banquet?" Max was the head chef in the hotel's restaurant which was renowned for its excellent cuisine and service.

Kelly nodded. That was all Charles needed to know. "Is Tina working the bar?"

"Yes, and Scott will be at the pool." Tina was one of the best bartenders in the Keys, with years of experience at the Ritz Carlton in Paris, and she was hot. Charles was pleased. Kelly was doing a great job setting everything up. He glanced at her, paying special attention to the top of her button-up shirt that showed just enough cleavage to turn his gaze more into a stare.

Kelly noticed it and blushed a little. Their eyes met, but they both immediately looked away. Sexual tension hung heavy in the air.

Charles cleared his throat and quickly changed the subject. The last thing he needed was to be connected to another sexual harassment case. Charles hadn't been able to resist flirting with Kelly's attractive predecessor, who had finally reported him to the hotel owner. That had almost led to him, Charles, being fired. He was lucky that Deanna, the former concierge, had taken a job offer somewhere else and dropped her charges.

"What's going on tomorrow morning?" he asked.

"For tomorrow morning, they booked a deep-sea fishing trip with Marlin Charter."

"Great choice. That'll keep them out of our hair for a while and give us time to clean up the resort," he said grinning. This group of tech executives from Silicon Valley had been there before. They had not only proven to be extremely demanding but were also heavy drinkers and very noisy. But they were exactly the type of big client the hotel urgently needed in these post-pandemic times.

Kelly grinned nervously. She had witnessed the group once before and knew what Charles meant. The last time an expensive old floor vase had been broken and one or two of the rooms had been destroyed quite a bit.

"And tomorrow night after the banquet they're going to Duval Street, right? So, let's hope they stay there and don't come back too early to party in the bar."

"Yes, and for the next morning, they have another boat rental. Some of them are divers. And then a couple of them depart the next evening, but most of them stay until Wednesday. We still need to check on their requested late checkouts."

Charles thought for a second and said: "I think you need to wait twenty-four hours after diving before you can fly. It has something to do with the pressure inside an airplane's cabin. You should check if any of the divers are departing the next morning."

Kelly nodded. She had already taken that into consideration. "That's why their flight is so late in the evening. It'll be over twenty-four hours after the last dive, even if the trip goes until five or six p.m.

8

Charles nodded pleased. Kelly knew what she was doing.

Chapter Three

L ittle Orchid Island was a gorgeous 25 acre private resort island, approximately 1,000 yards off-shore from Key West, where the Atlantic Ocean and Gulf of Mexico meet. The only way to reach the island was by boat. The hotel ran a ferry, which docked in front of the hotel's large canvas awning, leading to the main lobby. Though small and intimate, the Casa Bella was one of the incredibly beautiful hotels that Henry Flagler had built one hundred years ago. He was also the founder of the Florida East Coast Railway and builder of the Florida Overseas Railroad from Biscayne Bay to Key West.

The first mate assisted the guests onto the dock while the second mate handed the elegant designer luggage up to several bell boys who were placing the bags and suitcases onto luggage carts.

A group of ten from a renowned tech company in San Jose, eight men and two women, dressed in expensive casual designer clothes from Lululemon to Gucci to Golden Goose and Saint Laurent, climbed out of the boat onto the dock. Everyone was in high spirits and full of energy. They had obviously already been drinking heavily on the flight to the Keys. The group walked over to the pile of luggage and helped the bell boys sort their suitcases and carry-ons onto carts. The two women stood close to each other but didn't seem to be friends. Some dirty looks went back and forth.

One of the men walked ahead down the short dock, not paying attention to anything, and almost tripped over a rooster that was walking by and jumped away, clucking loudly.

Everyone laughed, so the man chimed in. "Love it. Cluck, cluck, cluck, cluck." He imitated the rooster and followed him a few steps.

Two younger attractive female hotel guests wearing tight shorts and tops with a bare midriff walked into the main lobby just as the group was arriving. The men looked at them nodding, elbowing each other, snickering.

Kelly and Charles were already standing at the entrance, ready to greet the guests. Kelly huffed and rolled her eyes secretly as she observed the men's behavior. She loved her job and helping hotel guests make the best of their vacations and keeping reality away from them a little, but this was seriously her least favorite group. They were rude, entitled, and downright arrogant. But, of course, the "customer was king," and Charles and Kelly greeted them with impeccable manners.

"Welcome to Little Orchid Island and the Casa Bella. I hope you had a great flight. I'm Charles, the general manager."

Kelly continued, "And I'm Kelly, your concierge.

We look forward to making the best of your vacation. Please feel free to contact me anytime you have any questions about activities on the island or trips in and around the Keys. The shuttle to the mainland departs every thirty minutes on the full and the half hour. And now please follow me to the front desk where you can check in. We did a pre-check-in, so your wait won't be too long."

Kelly and Charles walked ahead of the group through the beautiful lobby with dark wooden floors and heavy rattan furniture. Big Colonial-style fans created a cool breeze. Old framed black- and-white photos decorating the walls portrayed Henry Flagler and his third wife Mary Lily Kenan, showing scenes of the Florida Overseas Railroad being built and him boarding the first train to Key West on January 22, 1912.

The group followed Charles and Kelly to the front desk and looked around, impressed. Kelly took advantage of the brief silence. The beautiful lobby usually kept people stunned.

"Ladies and gentlemen, this is Claire, our front desk manager, and her team. They have your keys ready. All you need to do is present your credit cards and IDs for incidentals, and you'll be up to your rooms in no time."

"Welcome to the Casa Bella," said Claire, a middle-aged classy woman with a British accent. She wore big designer-glasses, impeccable make-up, and her naturally gray hair wasn't more than two or three inches long, cut to an edgy pixie cut. She had been working at the resort for twenty-five years and knew everything about it. "Please feel free to contact me with questions any time as well. We'll call your names up alphabetically. First is Adams, John?"

A young man, the second in charge behind the front desk, Kevin, called the second person, "Dumas, Lillian?"

It was a smooth operation, and the guests stepped up one by one, presenting their credit cards and IDs. Soon they were led up to their rooms by the bell boys. Kelly looked at the time on her phone and said to Charles, "Give it about five minutes, and the first calls will be coming in from people who don't have an oceanfront room but feel they should. Unfortunately, the company only paid for six oceanfront rooms, and the rest are facing the courtyard..." This was obviously a trip that the employees with the best annual revenue had won, fully paid for by their company.

Charles nodded, and Kelly was right; just a few minutes later, the phone at the front desk rang. One of the group members, Patrick Smith, called to complain that he didn't have an ocean view.

"I'm sorry, sir," said Claire, friendly yet firmly. "You have been assigned this room class by your travel agent. Unfortunately, all the oceanfront rooms are currently booked, otherwise I'd be glad to give you a free upgrade."

On the other end of the line, Mr. Smith was talking so loudly that Charles and Kelly could hear him through Claire's phone.

"There musht be a mistake! I was promised an

oceanfront room." Mr. Smith had obviously consumed a few drinks, as he slurred his words of protest.

"As I said, unfortunately, there's nothing I can do right now. Please feel free to check in with me tomorrow, I might be able to help you after checkout."

Patrick Smith muttered a few not-so-kind words and hung up. Claire looked toward Charles and Kelly and shrugged.

"Very well handled, Claire," said Charles. He turned toward Kelly, who was expected to stay for the course of the banquet. "So, are you going home now and returning later or are you staying?"

"I was going to go home and change into something more appropriate," replied Kelly, looking down at her plain button-up shirt and skirt.

"Okay, I'll see you later," he said. "Claire, I'll be in my office or room 101 if things get out of hand with Mr. Smith or anyone else. Please call me anytime." Room 101 was a suite that Charles reserved for himself whenever he had functions that required him to work late, and he couldn't make the last ferry to the mainland.

Meanwhile, some of the group had gathered at the pool bar. Scott and the other barkeepers were mixing cocktails as fast as they could. The group became louder and louder. Some other guests, annoyed by their noisy fellow guests, packed up their belongings and left, shaking their heads. Suddenly, there was a loud scream. One of the two women, Lillian Dumas, a pretty, tall blonde with a bit too much makeup, fell backward into the pool with a big splash.

Chapter Four

Lillian came up, coughing, choking, and spitting and waded over to the side of the pool with a disgusted, angry look on her face. She climbed out on the ladder, assisted by some of the men who had rushed over to help her. She was fuming. Her formerly-perfectly blow-dried long blonde hair hung down both sides of her face like corn husks. Her pretty little sundress was dripping and clung to her shapely body.

She marched straight up to the only other female in the group, Samantha, a redhead with short curly hair and freckles on a cute little nose, and pointed with her index finger, as she yelled, "You pushed me! And you'll pay for that!" She grabbed her key card and phone from the bar, turned around, and marched up to her room, leaving her shoes that were now floating in the pool. She was a pitiful sight, but some of the men couldn't help it and had to snicker.

Samantha watched her leave, more annoyed than anything. "I did not push you!" she yelled after Lillian, then asked the guy she had been flirting with, Lillian's boyfriend Ryan Goslan, who was Samantha's ex-boyfriend and she still had feelings for.

"I was talking to you the entire time, Ryan. Did you see me push Lillian into the pool?"

"I don't think so?" Ryan said quietly, but he didn't want to get in the middle of it. Women could be so catty, especially when they were fighting over him.

"That bitch has been doing nothing but complain ever since we departed," said Samantha. "It's probably karma because she's so negative and needy."

Nobody could tell what had really happened. Everyone was quite tipsy by now and nobody had paid attention. They finally concluded that Lillian had probably just fallen into the pool without being pushed but soon changed the subject. The next round of drinks was ready, and they all toasted to their upcoming vacation.

Kelly was just on her way home to go and change, when she ran into Lillian, barefoot and soaked, walking back to her room. Lillian was crying. She knew she wouldn't hear the end of this incident all weekend, especially from her "arch enemy" Samantha.

"Oh, no, what happened?" asked Kelly as she rushed up to her. "Is there anything I can do to help? Let me grab a towel for you. They're right over here."

Lillian lost it and started sobbing. "Someone... pushed... me... into the pool," she blurted out in between sobs. They were still close to the pool, and Kelly grabbed two fresh towels from the little towel cabana. She wrapped one around Lillian's shoulders in a comforting manner and handed her the other one for her face and hair.

"Why would anyone do that?" asked Kelly. "That's really mean. And you could have hit your head against the concrete or gotten some other injury."

"Could you please try to get my shoes out of the pool? They're probably ruined, but they're Christian Louboutin." Thinking of her $800 shoes floating in the pool made Lillian cry even harder.

"Oh, no, I'll try to fish them out or see if someone has already gotten them."

"Thanks. And thanks for the towels."

"What's your room number?" asked Kelly.

"Three ten."

Lillian continued walking up to her room, and Kelly headed toward the pool, rolling her eyes. There was always something. She had been looking forward to a nice hot shower and possibly even a quick nap, but now her break was being interrupted again. The group was laughing and causing quite a racket. Some of them stopped talking and examined Kelly who was not so unattractive herself with her long brunette hair and swimmer's physique. She looked in the pool. Nobody had bothered fishing the shoes out yet. *That's how these people care about their coworker*, Kelly thought gloomily.

The pool attendants were gone for the day, but Kelly knew where the telescopic pole with the net was, outside of the shack in the back of the bar. Kelly grabbed the pole that was hung up sideways along the wall and started fishing the shoes out, accompanied by the onlookers' annoying comments.

"Good job!"

"A bit more to the right!"

"Oh, she got it!"

Kelly wanted to turn around and ask them if they'd like to help, but it was a waste of time trying to talk to these people that were already quite drunk. They all cheered when she finally had the shoes. She hung the pole back up, grabbed the shoes, and waved goodbye with an attempt of a smile. Then she took the shoes straight to housekeeping.

"Hey, Linda," Kelly asked the housekeeper on duty. "Do you have anything I can stuff into these shoes to dry them out? They fell into the pool."

"Oh, no," said Linda. "They look quite destroyed."

"Yeah, what a waste. I'm sure they're very expensive," replied Kelly.

Linda grabbed a bunch of old newspapers from a shelf, crumbled a few pages up and stuffed them into the shoes. "That'll help pull out the moisture. Would you like me to take them up to the guest?" Linda asked.

"Thanks, Linda, but I'll take care of it. This group is important." She sighed, and they smiled at each other. They both knew their jobs were not for the faint of heart and that the guests always came first.

Kelly took the shoes up to Lillian's room. Lillian was quite sobered up and just mad now. "I know that someone pushed me, and I'm going to find out who it was. I think it was my boyfriend's ex-girlfriend Samantha," she said, her eyes gleaming angrily as she looked at her ruined shoes.

Kelly didn't know how Lillian intended on finding out, but she nodded. "I hope to see you at the banquet?"

"I certainly don't feel like going, but I'm not going to let someone ruin my fun," Lillian replied grimly.

Finally, Kelly took the shuttle to the mainland, got on her bike, and rode through the streets of Key West, past pretty pastel-colored conch houses, bigger Victorian homes, gift shops, boutique hotels, restaurants, ice cream and t-shirt shops. The early evening sun shone on her face, and she smiled as she casually pedaled along her daily route. She couldn't afford a car, but it wouldn't be practical to own one here anyhow. Parking was sparse in Key West, and everything was so close that a bike could get her anywhere within ten minutes. She loved her home in the Keys. She waved and greeted familiar faces as she drove by and was greeted back.

After a five-minute bike ride, Kelly took a right into a little cobblestone driveway, passing a stately light purple Victorian home with a beautiful overgrown yard and a straight row of tall palm trees in the front. She continued to the back of the house and stopped in front of a charming two-story guesthouse, almost a miniature of the main building, with two separate apartments, and parked her bike. The house belonged to the owners of the Casa Bella who were only in the country from time to time when they weren't traveling through Europe or vacationing in

Bali or Hawaii. They rented out the two back units exclusively to employees. Kelly entered the little guesthouse, walked down a hallway and up a staircase to the second floor and unlocked her front door. Due to the big windows, Kelly's little one-bedroom apartment had a lot of natural light, but it was shaded by some taller palm trees and a beautiful old gumbo limbo tree with sprawling branches. One of the best-known trees in the Florida Keys, gumbo limbos are sometimes jokingly referred to as the "tourist tree" because of their red peeling bark.

The apartment was neat and functionally decorated. Kelly wasn't a collector of knick-knacks and liked a clean and uncluttered environment. Since she was very organized, she had already planned what she would wear to the banquet tonight. A simple yet classy dark-green sleeveless linen shift dress hung from the doorframe leading to the bathroom. Underneath stood a pair of dark-green suede leather sandals. Even her underwear for tonight was already lying on the bed as well as a suede purse that matched the shoes and a pretty shell necklace. Kelly hopped into the shower in the tiny bathroom. She was just starting to relax under the stream of hot water as she lathered up with her favorite invigorating eucalyptus bodywash when her phone rang.

"Oh, damn," she mumbled to herself and tried to ignore it. But it kept ringing It must be important., she thought. She rinsed off, stepped out of the shower, wrapped a towel around herself and another one around her hair, and walked back into the bedroom to grab the phone. There were three missed calls from Charles.

Oh, no, that can't be good, she thought and punched in Charles' number on speed dial to return his call.

Chapter Five

W hat was so important that Charles had to
call Kelly three times and couldn't wait
until she was back at the Casa Bella? Kelly
tried calling him back, but now he wasn't answering
his phone, and it went straight to voicemail. Kelly left
a message.

"Hi, Charles, it's Kelly. I'm sorry I missed your
calls. Since there seems to be something urgent, I'm
changing now and heading back to the hotel. Please
call me back as soon as you get this."

Kelly thanked her lucky stars that she had already
gotten her outfit ready this morning. She stepped into
the dress, brushed her hair, and put on some light
makeup as fast as she could. She grabbed her bike and
made her way back to the Casa Bella, a delightful sight
in her pretty dark-green dress and suede pumps. Her
long brunette hair flowed behind her in the tropical
evening breeze.

Stepping on her brakes and coming to a stop, she
jumped off her bike and pushed it into the bike rack
next to the little dock where the shuttle to Little Orchid
Island departed. An ambulance with flashing lights

sat at the dock, and someone on a stretcher was being lifted out of the boat and pushed into the back of the ambulance by two paramedics. Obviously, logistics to get to and from Little Orchid Island weren't great in case of emergencies. Quickly, Kelly walked up to Charles, who also climbed out of the boat and was about to get in the back of the ambulance to accompany the guest to the hospital.

"I'm glad you're here," he said as Kelly walked up to him with a worried expression on her face. "One of the group members, Ken Miller, fell down the stairs leading to the lobby, believe it or not. He says he was pushed."

"What?" Kelly exclaimed flabbergasted. "How badly is he injured?"

Charles looked at her. "It looks like he might have broken a leg, but they need to do some x-rays first. He might also have a concussion. Sorry for calling you. I need to go to the hospital with him and wanted one of us to be here while the banquet starts. I'll keep you posted. You might have to hold my speech if I don't make it back on time."

Kelly nodded. "Charles, before I left, one of the two women fell into the pool, and she also said someone pushed her. Isn't that strange?"

The ambulance was about to depart. "That *is* strange. Let's talk about it later, I've got to go." Charles climbed into the back, and the ambulance left with flashing lights.

Alex, the shuttle's captain, made a special trip for Kelly, and she was quickly taken over to the island.

She walked into the lobby. Two of the group members, already dressed for the banquet in slacks and nice button-up shirts, stepped up to her. "Kelly, do you know what happened to Ken?"

"It seems he fell down those stairs," she pointed at the curved main wooden staircase behind the elevator, leading up to the second and third floors. "He might have broken his leg. I'll keep you posted as soon as I hear something. Charles, the general manager, is at the hospital with him." Kelly didn't say anything about Ken's accusation of being pushed, just like Lillian. She didn't want to cause too much commotion before she spoke with Charles.

People were coming down and gathering in front of the restaurant, which faced the ocean on the opposite side of the lobby from the front desk.

The banquet was about to start. Kelly looked nervously at her phone. She'd have to make some type of announcement with news on Ken and didn't know what to say before she heard from Charles. Lillian, her hair "fixed," and wearing a pretty, sequined dress and strappy sandals, stepped out of the elevator with Ryan, looking around a bit insecurely. But everybody had already forgotten about the pool incident. The new one was more exciting. Everyone was wondering what had happened, and the word was already out that Ken had accused someone of pushing him. Finally, Kelly's phone rang. It was Charles. She stepped aside and answered the call.

"Hi, Charles, any news?"

"Yes, his leg is indeed broken. Unfortunately, it's a

complicated fracture and needs surgery. So, he needs to stay overnight. Surgery is scheduled for tomorrow morning. He's still thinking about whether he wants to involve the police and press charges or not. Please just inform the group that he won't be back tonight, but don't say anything about his accusations. I'll be back in about half an hour."

"Okay, talk to you later."

Kelly turned around. Everyone was in the restaurant and had taken their seats around two big round tables. Lillian made a bit of a fuss because she didn't want to sit at Samantha's table, but the issue was resolved quickly, when one of the men who liked Samantha volunteered to trade seats. Servers brought out cocktails and appetizer platters. Kelly stepped next to the bar, grabbed a cocktail from one of the trays, cleared her throat, and said, "Ladies and gentlemen..." Finally, everyone quieted down and listened. "I'm sorry to announce that your colleague Ken has indeed fractured his leg and is going to require surgery tomorrow. He'll be in the hospital for another night. Visiting hours are posted on their website if you want to try and visit him."

Surprised, everyone started talking at the same time. Kelly interrupted them. "Nevertheless, I hope the rest of you can make the best of your stay. I hope you have a pleasant time and make some fun memories. Enjoy your dinner, prepared by one of the most renowned chefs in the Keys, Max Freeman."

Everyone clapped or clinked their forks against their glasses as the servers brought in little cups of lobster bisque and placed them in front of the guests. Kelly supervised things for a few minutes, then peeked into the kitchen where her friend and guesthouse neighbor, Max, was working fully concentrated and giving instructions to his staff. He was known to run a tight ship but was also very popular and had a keen sense of humor.

He saw Kelly and blew her a kiss. She waved, smiled briefly, and pulled her head back out so as not to distract him. Max had become a special friend who felt like a brother to Kelly, and they went out whenever they could or just met on Kelly's balcony or Max's porch for a morning coffee or evening beer and poured their hearts out to each other.

Little did Kelly know that Max's feelings were a little deeper than that, but he hid it well since she didn't seem to want more than a platonic friendship and camaraderie.

As soon as Kelly had made sure that everything was running smoothly, she sat down and had a lobster bisque herself. She was starving and could already feel the dizzying effects of the alcohol. Max had surpassed himself again with his cooking skills. The lobster bisque was to die for. It was rich and flavorful, a pureed cream-based soup with giant chunks of fresh Florida lobster. After a few more drinks, it didn't take long for the group to be back in its usual party mode again. They yelled from table to table, joking and partying it up. Even though they were noisy, Kelly could tell that they were having a good time, and that's what everyone wanted.

Just as the main course, a choice of surf and turf or pan-seared grouper, was being served, Charles stepped into the restaurant. Everyone looked up, expecting an update, but he stepped next to Kelly and said, "Enjoy your dinner, ladies and gentlemen, I'll give you an update when you're done with your meals. Ken is fine."

Everyone nodded, distracted by the delicious steaming plates in front of them and nodded. The room was quiet for a few minutes as the party enjoyed their meal.

Max, a tall lanky young man with longer curly blonde hair and thick glasses, stepped out of the kitchen and walked toward Kelly and Charles with two plates of surf and turf. He wore his chef hat that currently hid most of his face and a white apron wrapped around his waist that wasn't very white anymore. He beamed and blushed a little as he set down the plates in front of Kelly and Charles and said, "Enjoy!"

Kelly smiled at him and thanked him profusely. "Wow, Max, this looks really great. Thank you very much." There was an entire Florida lobster tail on each plate, a piece of medium-rare, seared filet mignon with a piece of butter and some sprigs of rosemary and thyme on it as well as a little dish of melted butter for the lobster. The dish was rounded up by some fresh oven-roasted green beans. Kelly and Charles realized they were starving and didn't have to be told twice before they attacked their plates. For a moment, before returning to the kitchen, Max threw the VT Tech group a dirty look, but nobody paid attention to him.

Chapter Six

After a small break the dessert was brought out, a classic key lime pie with a thick layer of meringue and a delicious graham cracker crust. Max didn't even bother trying to top his friends' pie from the Key Lime Pie Co. and just ordered it from there and spruced it up with some fresh berries and whipped cream. Once again, everyone in the restaurant quieted down. Just some oohs and aahs and "this is to die for" were to be heard.

A couple of the group headed back to the pool bar, but most of them went out front to catch the boat shuttle to the mainland and Duval Street, where the main nightlife in Key West took place and could be crazy at times.

"Well, it looks like most of them are headed downtown," said Charles, very pleased as he smiled at Kelly. "We could use the business in the bar, but at least we don't have to put up with their shenanigans."

"I hope they remember that our last shuttle departs at one a.m. from the mainland," she replied shaking her head, ready for more trouble.

"I'll remind them."

Charles got up and tapped his fork against his glass.

"Hi everyone, can I have a word, please?" People who were already departing the restaurant stopped in their tracks and turned around to listen to him. "This is a friendly reminder that the last shuttle returning to Little Orchid Island departs at one a.m. from the dock across from the Hyatt Hotel. No exceptions. The captain goes home afterwards, and the boat is anchored for the night. And, whoever booked the deep-sea fishing trip tomorrow morning, please remember that you depart at eight a.m. Breakfast is served from seven till ten right here and on the porch. Have a nice rest of your evening."

They stormed out like teenagers who had never been out drinking and behaved that way too.

That was the last thing Kelly remembered of that evening.

Back to present time / next morning

Kelly stared at Samantha Berg's body in shock. "We have to inform Charles!" she said, gasping for air. "Don't touch anything. Can you please call him, Mary? He's in room 101. I'll call the police."

A couple of minutes later, Charles came sprinting

down to the pool, also a few hotel guests had heard the commotion and came up to see what was going on. Lillian stepped up with her boyfriend Ryan. Kelly saw the almost satisfied look on her face and wondered if Lillian was the one who had pushed Samantha off her balcony. But kill someone as revenge for pushing her into the pool? That didn't make any sense unless Lillian was a coldblooded murderer.

Soon Detective Bianca Sanchez, born and raised in Miami, but originally of Columbian descent and her colleague, Detective Michael Brinkmann, a middle-aged stout Bavarian with thick salt and pepper hair and a thick moustache of the same color, arrived. Charles wrung his hands as he greeted his old friends. Everyone knew everybody in Key West, and Charles and Kelly had dealt with Officers Brinkmann and Sanchez in the past. "Guys, can we keep this on the down low, please? This is bad press for the hotel, and the owners will be horrified."

"Morning, Charles. Well, be assured that the press won't hear anything from us," replied Officer Sanchez as she shook Charles' and then Kelly's hand. "But what do you think happened here?" It was more a rhetorical question because it was obvious what had happened. They both took a closer look at the body. "So, do we have ID on the victim?" Sanchez asked.

"Yes, Samantha Berg, a guest here with a group from the company VT Tech from San Jose, California," replied Charles. "A gift from their company because they're the top 10 salespeople or something like that."

"No signs of trauma to her wrists," said Bianca as

she took a closer look at the body. "I'm trying to imagine whether she fought with someone and was then pushed off the balcony. She obviously fell backwards on her head, as you can see from this big wound," he pointed at a wound on the back of her head, "so her torso could have been pushed from the front." Suddenly, Bianca called into the crowd of hotel guests. "Whoever knew the victim personally, could you please step forward?" Lillian stepped forward. "Well, we all did, she was our colleague. But I don't think she was best friends with anyone here." Brinkmann and Sanchez looked at each other. That didn't sound like Samantha Berg had been very popular.

"Do you know if she suffered from depression?"

"You mean did she kill herself? I don't think so," replied Lillian. "She was quite full of herself and always in a good mood. At least as far as I can tell."

Not a very nice way to speak of the dead, thought Kelly.

"Well, we're going to have to wait for our medical examiner, Thomas Bernard, he's on his way from Marathon," said Brinkmann to Charles. We'll cover her up for now but can't move her until he gets here. We'd appreciate if you could clear out the onlookers and keep this area closed off for now. Bianca and I will look at her room and the balcony. Can you please get a room key for us?"

Charles nodded, got the master key out of his pocket that he always carried while at work and showed it to the officers. Then, eager to keep operations running, he asked Bianca, "Is it okay if these men still go on the deep-sea fishing trip they booked, or do we need to cancel? They'll be back in the late afternoon."

Bianca nodded. "We'll figure out who we need to question in the next few hours. No need to keep them all sitting around all day."

Charles looked at the onlookers, mostly members of the VT Tech Group. "Folks, please decide whether you want to go on your deep-sea fishing trip or not. I know this is a shock, but maybe you should make the best of your stay anyhow and go about your day. There's nothing we can do right now. The police might have to question you later, so please be on standby and check your messages when you return."

Kelly chimed in. "Whoever is still going, please get ready and meet us out front at the boat shuttle at eight a.m."

They all looked at each other insecurely, but most of the men left to go on the fishing trip. Lillian grabbed a coffee and some fruit from the breakfast buffet and sat down on the patio. She had planned on spending the day at the pool and then going shopping.

Kelly said quietly to Officers Sanchez and Brinkmann, "I don't want to make any accusations, but the victim and that lady over there, Lillian Dumas, seemed to not get along very well. Lillian fell into the pool yesterday and accused Samantha of pushing her. Lillian was *really* upset and said Samantha would pay for it. Samantha used to be together with Lillian's boyfriend, Ryan Goslan. There might still be some love triangle going on. Also, one of the members of the group fell down the stairs yesterday and broke his leg. He said someone pushed him as well."

Brinkmann and Sanchez exchanged a glance. There was certainly some type of pattern going on.

"Thanks for this info," replied Bianca. "So, do these people all belong to a group that came together?" Charles and Kelly nodded. "They're the top ten executives from VT Tech in San Jose," said Kelly. Sanchez looked at Kelly. "Do you know what would be very helpful? We need a list of all the people in that group and their room and cell phone numbers. Is that something you could work on for us?"

Kelly nodded and walked toward the front desk. She realized that she still hadn't had a chance to go home and change and sighed.

Chapter Seven

Gilda Gomez, the middle-aged Cuban florist who took care of all the flower and orchid arrangements at the hotel, was working on a few new big arrangements in the lobby as Kelly stepped in. The two women weren't close but chatted from time to time when Kelly wasn't too busy. Right now, Kelly was in a rush to get to the front desk and complete her assignment for the police officers. But she greeted Gilda and still had time to notice the beautiful tropical flowers Gilda was arranging in six matching vases for the six matching tables in the lobby. The tall colorful stems of ginger, heliconia, anthurium and bird of paradise perfectly complemented the lobby's tropical design.

"Good morning, Gilda, gorgeous flowers!"

"Buenos dias, beautiful. What's going on, Chica? You look pale. Are you not feeling well today?" Gilda had a sixth sense and knew when something was wrong. She stuck an orchid bloom in Kelly's hair to cheer her up.

"Not a good day, Gilda. See all the commotion back there by the pool? One of the guests fell off a balcony to their death last night. Police are there right now investigating her death."

"¡Dios mio! My God!" Gilda was shocked. "Did she jump or was she murdered?"

"Nobody knows yet."

"Well, we all know this hotel is haunted," Gilda said matter-of-factly. "I've always been surprised that nothing has happened in the past couple of years. One of a famous local author's "female companions" supposedly committed suicide here by jumping off her balcony and used to be seen wandering on the patio and up and down the hallways during the full moon."

Gilda would have gone on and on, but Kelly interrupted her. "Sorry, Gilda. I need to get some info for the police from the front desk. They're waiting."

"You should tell them this place is haunted," added Gilda as Kelly started walking away.

Kelly nodded in a non-committal manner. "I'll talk to you later." She thought this was some old wives' tale and didn't believe in ghosts. That statement made Gilda seem a bit crazy.

Gilda continued working on her flower arrangements but kept a sharp eye on the police officers on the back patio. She recognized Officer Sanchez. Gilda had helped solve a few crimes in the past and was very interested in what was going on here. As a young woman in Cuba, she had started training at a police academy and had seen herself as an "inspectora" one day. But then her family had fled the dictatorship in the country, and she never had the chance to continue going to school in the United States and then got married and had kids. After her kids had grown up and her husband had passed away, leaving her as a young widow, Gilda had started a plant-sitting business for upscale homes and provided local hotels with flowers and arrangements. She also ran the Key West Garden Club and volunteered at the local Orchid Society. Her job didn't make her rich, but she was able to pay the bills and enjoyed what she did. From time to time, though, the old dream of being a sleuth returned like a flame inside of her that never entirely went out. Gilda could be quite helpful for the police with her contacts all over town, especially in the Cuban community. Bianca Sanchez was aware of this and asked her for assistance every now and then. Sometimes, Gilda had to be told to back off because, like a terrier, she wouldn't let go once she got wound up in something. She didn't have the proper training and needed to let the professionals do their jobs.

Gilda stared through the window and forgot to even pretend she was working on her flowers. She'd find out what was going on. Kelly, on her way back, noticed that Gilda seemed to be on another planet. "Is everything okay, Gilda?"

Gilda flinched and returned to reality. "Oh, sorry, I just zoned out for a minute." She changed the subject.

"You look so nice today. Is something special going on?"

Kelly looked down at her dress and blushed a little. She had to go home, take a shower, and change into some normal clothes but probably wouldn't have a chance until lunch.

"No, I was late this morning and just grabbed it," she lied. She'd forgotten about the Charles incident. Her headache returned as she thought about it.

After handing officer Sanchez the list with names, phone numbers and room numbers of the tech group members, she looked at her phone and realized it was time for the participants of the deep-sea fishing trip to depart.

"Charles, do you want to come and see off the deep-sea fishers or shall I take care of it?"

Usually, she would've taken care of this by herself, but with this group, everything was different and delicate. Especially now.

He looked at her and decided, "I'll come with you." As they walked out to the boat shuttle departure and arrival area in front of the resort, he acted normal and noncommittal. Kelly wondered whether he even remembered what had happened last night. She was going to have to say something. But not now.

Five of the eight men in the group were waiting at the boat shuttle to go on the deep-sea fishing trip. One was in the hospital, probably in surgery right now, the two others hadn't signed up to go fishing and were relaxing in the hotel. The boat pulled up with Medical

Examiner Thomas Bernard on board. The first mate threw a rope, and the bell boy caught it and fastened it around the dock cleats. Then Bernard jumped out of the boat and the five men got in.

"We'll see you guys later. Have a great catch." Kelly wished the men good luck as Charles greeted Bernard, a tall bald man in his early forties who wasn't handsome in a typical manner but had some sort of sex appeal that made women look twice. Kelly was fascinated by his piercing blue eyes and his keen aura of confidence and couldn't stop staring at him.

Charles and Kelly led Bernard to the body. The pool area had been taped off with yellow "crime scene" tape. A police officer was keeping unauthorized visitors out but lifted the tape and respectfully greeted Bernard as he walked up. Bernard shook Brinkmann and Sanchez's hands, put on a pair of latex gloves and kneeled next to the body. He carefully removed the tarp, examined dead Samantha, and took some pictures. With a very serious face and full of concentration, he looked at her from every angle and turned around and looked up at the balconies. In his mind he reenacted how the accident or murder could have taken place.

"Can you already guesstimate the time of death?" asked officer Brinkmann.

Bernard looked up at Brinkmann and Sanchez with his piercing blue eyes.

"Yes, around three a.m. I'll be able to say more as soon as I've examined her in my lab. Please let the officers know they can take her there now. Can I see the room and balcony where this happened?" he asked.

Kelly noted that Bernard didn't speak with the uniformed cops but only with Brinkmann and Sanchez. He looked like a medical examiner out of a movie.

The officers zipped a body bag around Samantha and carried it toward the dock where it was to be transported to the mainland and picked up by a hearse.

Officers Brinkmann and Sanchez and Bernard looked at Charles, asking him to accompany them upstairs to Samantha's room.

As Bianca was quickly giving her team some instructions, Charles looked at Kelly and suddenly seemed to notice that she was wearing the same clothes as last night and remembered what had happened between them.

"Since the group is gone and I don't need you here right now, why don't you take a break and go home to freshen up, Kelly?" he said quietly so that the police officers couldn't hear him.

Their eyes met, and the atmosphere was extremely awkward for a moment. Kelly nodded as Charles turned around and walked away with the officers.

Kelly would've loved to eavesdrop on what the police saw and said upstairs, but the adrenaline that had kept her going had suddenly disappeared, and she realized how exhausted and hungry she was.

Chapter Eight

Kelly quickly went and checked the messages at her desk in the lobby. There was nothing that couldn't wait until the afternoon. Then she grabbed her purse and walked over to the dock to take the shuttle to the mainland.

Gilda was standing there as well, waiting for the shuttle. She was pulling a big shopping cart on wheels behind her with some leftover flowers and her gardening tools inside. She beamed over her whole face as she discovered Kelly, fished some flowers out of her cart, arranged them a little and handed them to Kelly.

"Why don't you take these to your place. They will brighten your day."

"Oh, that's so nice of you, Gilda. I can really use a little pick me up right now. It's been quite a strange last twenty-four hours. I don't even know if I want to work here anymore."

Gilda nodded.

"You know, freelancing is always a good option. I have a friend who freelances as a concierge. She shops for guests before they arrive in their condos, organizes trips and dinners for them, and she's quite successful. She also covers in some hotels while the concierges are on vacation. You're your own boss and you can work as much or as little as you want."

Kelly nodded. That sounded interesting. She couldn't imagine not having all the great benefits she got at the Casa Bella, but today she just didn't feel like going back.

She looked out toward Key West and then down into the water as the boat chugged along and left Little Orchid Island behind them. The water was a crystal-clear aquamarine blue, and Kelly watched some beautiful parrotfish right underneath the surface as they darted through the water, following the boat.

Kelly looked at Gilda who was happily chattering with the captain. Maybe Gilda was right. Maybe it was time for a change. As soon as the ferry had arrived at the dock, Kelly said goodbye to Gilda and started riding home on her bike, the flowers in a basket in the front. Even though she was tired and hungover and needed a shower badly, Kelly loved this daily ride home on her bike. Where else would she be living in such a sub-tropical smalltown environment with beautiful overgrown front yards and narrow cobblestone roads with chickens darting back and forth? She passed the Southernmost Point, an anchored concrete buoy, marking the southernmost point in the continental United States, with tourists lined up to take each other's pictures. Then she took a right onto Whitehead Street and passed the

Hemingway House, former home of Ernest Hemingway, which was now a museum. The guesthouse that she lived in was located a few more houses down the road. If she quit her job, she'd have to give that up too. It was only rented out to employees of the hotel.

Kelly took a right into the beautiful overgrown driveway lined with hibiscus and bougainvillea shrubs and looked at the pretty villa and guesthouse in the back. Max's bike was parked in the bike rack. He usually didn't start working until noon since the hotel's restaurant wasn't open for lunch. She parked her bike, walked upstairs, stuck the flowers from Gilda into a pretty vase, gulped down a cold glass of water to hydrate, then she jumped right under the hot shower. The hot water felt relaxing and soothing. A few minutes later she stepped out, refreshed but tired. She looked at the time on her phone. There was still enough time for a quick cat nap before she had to head back to the hotel. Kelly set her alarm for twenty minutes but slept straight through it. She was woken up by someone knocking at the door.

"Just a second!" she yelled as she quickly slipped into a simple t-shirt dress and walked over to the door.

It was Max, holding two cups of coffee. He smiled. "I heard you coming and thought you could use a cup of coffee after last night." Kelly smiled back at him.

"Oh Max, you're the best friend. That's really what I need right now, and thanks for waking me up. I was about to oversleep. I need to head back in half an hour. Isn't that when your shift starts too?"

Max nodded. "Yup."

He handed Kelly the coffee and they both sat down on two folding chairs on the little balcony with an antique ornamental metal railing in front of Kelly's apartment.

She looked at him. "Do you have the slightest idea what happened last night or this morning? One of the two women in the group from last night fell off her balcony and is dead."

Max almost burnt himself and choked on his coffee. "What?! How could that happen?"

"There's something crazy going on with that group. The other woman fell into the pool yesterday and said she was pushed, one of the guys fell down the stairs right before the banquet and now this. That can't be a coincidence. Someone is attacking these people."

"It sounds like it. Which one is dead?"

"Samantha Berg."

Max shook his head in disbelief. "That's unbelievable."

"Gilda thinks the hotel is haunted."

"I've actually heard those rumors too."

"But isn't that a little crazy?"

"I dunno. There's proof that various people have seen a famous Key West author's mistress wandering around the hotel. I don't really believe it either, but…"

"Let's google it," Kelly replied. She picked up her phone and googled *Is the Casa Bella on Little Orchid Island haunted?* A few articles came up about the death of a famous Key West author's mistress and how several people had seen her wandering through the Casa Bella, long after her death.

"Well, it does sound creepy," said Kelly, "but why would the ghost suddenly show up when this group is here? She hasn't been seen in years."

"It does sound crazy," replied Max. He took a sip of coffee and thought for a minute. "Could there be competition between the members of the group because they all want to be the employee of the year or so?"

"And now one of them is killing the other nine?" It didn't make sense either. How would that person expect not to get caught?

Max looked at the time on his phone. "Well, I have to get ready for work."

"Oh, and Max, can I ask you something?" Kelly hated bringing it up, but she really needed more information about what might have happened last night.

"Sure, what's up?"

"I think I blacked out last night. Did you see me do anything crazy or did anyone else say something? I really need to know what happened."

Max didn't know either if he should really tell her, because she had been quite out of it. But then he decided to be honest.

"Yeah, you were quite drunk and flirted with Charles quite a bit. You guys left together..."

"Oh my gosh, Max, someone must have put a roofie in my drink. I'd have never done that! My boss! I feel like I can't even face him anymore."

Max didn't comment. He was even more upset about the whole situation because he liked Kelly, and she obviously didn't reciprocate. Then he swallowed, looked at her and said, "Be careful. Remember what happened to your predecessor. You're going to be blamed and not Charles."

Kelly's face was as white as a sheet. She just sat there, staring at Max. He was right.

Chapter Nine

Kelly and Max rode their bikes back to the resort together. The sun shone on their faces as they raced over to the boat shuttle. They still somehow managed to have a conversation from bike to bike, more yelling than talking. For a small moment, they both seemed cheerful and carefree, and everyone who didn't know them would have guessed they were a happy couple.

Things could be so easy. But Kelly didn't seem to want easy. *Why did everything always have to be so complicated?* Max thought as he watched Kelly push her bike into the bike rack and lock it. They got along so well, but she didn't seem to have the same feelings he had for her. He was very much attracted to her and could have hung out with her all day, but she seemed to be looking for something more complicated…

They both jumped into the waiting boat and greeted the captain and first mate. Kelly was already nervous because she'd have to face Charles soon. Either he or she was going to have to mention last night. Her face already felt hot and red just thinking about it.

Max and Kelly stepped off the boat; Kelly walked toward the main entrance and the lobby, while Max headed around the building to the kitchen entrance.

"Have a nice day," they both said, almost simultaneously, and laughed. Again, Max looked a little too long, but Kelly didn't notice.

Charles had already checked on her several times. There was a note on her desk that said: *Please call me as soon as you get this. Charles.* Kelly's heart started racing. She sat to calm down for a second, looking out the window at the palm trees swaying in the wind, the beautiful ocean right behind them. Small white bits of spray crested the waves. The daily afternoon storm was brewing again. Kelly inhaled and exhaled a few times. Then she was ready to face Charles. She got up, straightened her skirt, and walked through the lobby and down the hallway with a sign that said:

For Employees Only.

Kelly paused briefly and took a deep breath, but then she lifted her hand and knocked on the door.

"Come in!"

Kelly mustered all her courage, opened the door, and stuck her head inside.

"Do you have a moment?"

"Yes, please come in." Charles jumped up from behind his big wooden desk, walked toward a leather seating arrangement and gestured for Kelly to sit down across from him.

For a moment, Charles just sat there, staring at her legs. He didn't quite know how to say what he wanted to say either. Kelly felt terribly uncomfortable and wanted to pull her skirt longer to cover her legs. Then Charles finally cleared his throat and said: "Kelly, what happened yesterday..."

In that same instance, there was a brief knock at the door. Charles' wife Liz and two of their three kids, Tina, four, and Charles Jr., two, walked in without waiting for a reply. The oldest daughter, Lynne, was in school.

"Daddy, Daddy!" yelled the kids simultaneously, and both ran through the room and jumped onto Charles' lap. They recognized Kelly and said, "Hey, Kelly!"

Liz was hesitant and remained at the office's entrance, taking in the way Charles and Kelly were sitting there in an almost intimate manner. At least, that's how she interpreted the situation.

"We assumed last night was long and brought you some coffee and croissants," said Liz, nodding at a little Starbucks carrier she held in her hand. She set the goodies down on the desk and frowned, wondering if Kelly's evening, and night, had been long too.

Kelly jumped up. She didn't want to bother the little family and it was a good way out of the prickly situation for now. "I should really get back to work. Nice to see you, Liz, kids," she said as she nodded at Liz and quickly walked out of the office. She walked away as fast as she could but still heard them start to argue.

Kelly sat back down at her desk and held her hands up to her face, trying to cool her burning red cheeks with her hands. The headache was coming back with full force. She couldn't stay in this situation, but even if she quit right now, she'd have a two-week-notice period and would probably have to train her successor. But then she remembered: she had a week of vacation left. A deep sultry voice interrupted her thoughts. "Miss, can I ask you some questions?"

A woman in her mid-fifties with straightened bleached blonde hair, a floppy hat and a short pink Lilly Pulitzer beach cover-up had stepped up to Kelly's desk and was looking through some brochures.

Kelly was lost in her thoughts again and came back to reality when the woman addressed her. "Oh, I'm so sorry! I was daydreaming there for a second."

"It seems like everyone here is having kind of a bad day today," the lady replied, nodding at the pool area where some police officers were still working and not letting guests enter the pool area.

"I'm so sorry that this is happening during your vacation," replied Kelly, glad to be distracted with work.

"Do we know what happened yet? I was going to spend the afternoon by the pool."

"No, only that she fell. It's a mystery whether she was pushed or whether it was an accident..."

Kelly tried to change the subject. She didn't feel comfortable discussing the incident with a guest and was probably not supposed to.

"You know, we have a sister property on the south side of Key West," she continued, "you are allowed to use the amenities there as well. Also, I'd like to give you a gift card that you can use on our entire property for the inconvenience of our pool being closed today. May I ask your name?"

"Marilyn McGaffy. I'm in the Palm Suite."

Marilyn took the gift card that Kelly handed her and looked at the name tag on her desk. "Thanks, Kelly." She was very nosy though and didn't want to change the subject.

"So, did someone else in the same group really have an accident too? And the other woman belonging to the group got pushed into the pool yesterday?"

"Well, we don't know yet..."

"May I ask where the group is going deep-sea fishing today?"

Kelly took a closer look at Marilyn. Why was this lady so interested in what was going on with the group? That seemed rather strange.

"Are you affiliated with them somehow?" Kelly asked carefully to not be unfriendly to the guest.

"No, just curious. Well, thanks for the gift card. I've got to go. Nice chatting with you. I might be back for other recommendations. I've heard the Hemingway House is nice, too." Without waiting for Kelly to reply, she turned around and exited the lobby through the back door leading to the pool and the oceanfront rooms.

At the same time, Liz and the kids walked through the lobby toward the exit. Liz was almost dragging Charles Jr., who was moping and didn't want to leave.

"I wanna stay and play with Daddy," he whined

as his mom pulled him along.

Tina freed herself from her mother's hand, ran up to Kelly's desk and said, "Hi, Miss Kelly! Can we draw?"

Kelly had drawn with her the last time they were here, and Tina remembered.

"Come on, Tina," called Liz impatiently.

She threw such a dirty look at Kelly that she would have dropped dead if looks could kill. Kelly felt awful. She was now a homewrecker. Her decision was made. She had to leave and end whatever had happened with Charles.

Chapter Ten

As Liz and the kids walked through the lobby toward the hotel's exit, Kelly opened a new document, typed something on her desktop computer and printed it. She grabbed the document from the printer's feeder and proofread it as she walked over to Charles' office. She knocked, opened the door, and entered without even waiting for an answer.

Charles was still sitting at his desk the way Liz had left him: upset, holding his head in his hands, his eyes closed, feeling sorry for himself after Liz had accused him of cheating on her yet again. And she was right. Even though nothing had happened between him and Kelly last night, Charles knew something would have happened if she hadn't passed out or it was about to happen soon. He knew there was something wrong with him because he had to prove to himself again and again what a "man" he was.

Kelly slammed the document on his desk and walked back out of the room. He picked up the piece of paper and read Kelly's letter of resignation. His hand with the letter dropped down to the desk and he just sat there for a while, feeling miserable. The whole world seemed to be mad at him, but he knew it was his own fault.

Charles liked Kelly. He knew he had gone too far again, but Kelly seemed like the type of woman who'd be able to forget about last night and be able to continue working with him on a professional basis. He only thought about himself and didn't feel like having to find a new concierge yet again. He got up and quickly caught up with her as she walked down the hallway.

"Kelly, can we please talk?"

"Sorry, Charles," Kelly replied shortly. "I'm putting in my two weeks' notice, and there's nothing you can do to change my mind. I don't know what happened between us last night, but I do know it went too far. I'm considering telling the police that someone might have put a roofie in one of my drinks."

Front desk manager Claire, who was coming out of the accounting office, saw what was going on. She took a step backward into the office, quietly closing the door but holding her ear up to the door, eavesdropping.

"What are you talking about? Do you seriously think someone here would have done that?" That was a terrible accusation.   Charles whispered a bit too loudly and tried to grab her arm and hold her back. Full of determination, Kelly shook his hand off and kept walking back to her desk. She was a professional and would stay here until she could start her vacation next week, but she wasn't going to change her mind.

She hated the feelings she even now still had for Charles and couldn't live with that, thinking of his three little kids and his wife.

Kelly felt that every single person in the hotel lobby, both guests and front desk personnel, was now silently staring at her and Charles, who had followed her, but she didn't care. She grabbed her purse and walked out the front door, her eyes welling up with tears.

Meanwhile, Officers Brinkmann and Sanchez and some forensics officers were still searching Samantha Berg's room and balcony for any hints or evidence. Bianca stood on the balcony, visualizing how the accident or murder could have taken place. There were bits and pieces of a broken champagne flute on the tile floor of the balcony as well as two flowerpots that had obviously been knocked over. In Bianca's mind, Samantha, holding a glass of champagne in her hand, was arguing with someone. Her back leaning against the balcony railing, then the other person, who must've been quite strong, suddenly gave her a hard shove. Bianca saw the two pots falling over, Samantha trying to catch her balance for a moment, but then flying down in slow motion.

Michael called out from the bathroom: "Look what I found, guys!" He waved a box of bupropion, a strong antidepressant, that he had just found at the bottom of Samantha's cosmetic bag. "So, suicide is an option if she was taking these. Let me see if the prescribing doctor's name is on here." He took a closer look at the box that was almost empty and called one of the officers at the police station. "Claudia, please get me the number of a doctor in Cupertino, Dr. Manuel Bockhorn. It seems our victim suffered from depression, and we need to question her doctor about the severity of her illness."

For Michael, the case was now solved after finding the antidepressants, but Bianca was not so sure. The traces of a fight with the broken glass and the knocked-over pots were too obvious. Someone committing suicide wouldn't make such a mess and leave a farewell note.

"I want to question the guests in this hallway and the neighboring rooms about what they saw or heard." She picked up the room phone and called Charles, who was back in his office. "Charles, can we please get a list of the people in the rooms close to the victim's room? I need to question them."

Charles replied, "Sure," hung up and called the front desk. Minutes later, he was upstairs and handed Bianca a list of guests in rooms close to Samantha's on the third floor. Samantha's ex-boyfriend, Ryan Goslan, was right next door to her room, and next to his room was Lillian's. So, Ryan could have had access to both rooms...

Another member of the group was right across from her, Patrick Smith, the man who had complained that he didn't have an oceanfront room, but he was currently on the deep-sea fishing trip. Two other guests across the hallway weren't in their rooms. It was hard to reach people while they were on vacation. The people in the room on the other side of Samantha's, an older couple from Orlando, hadn't heard or seen anything. The crime had happened in the middle of the night, and they had been fast asleep. The woman was crying, shocked about what had happened in the night right next to their room, and now she changed her mind and wasn't sure whether she had had voices arguing or not. *This is leading nowhere*, thought Bianca. She thanked the couple and stepped back into Samantha's room.

"Let's call the hospital and check if the guy who broke his leg last night is out of surgery yet. I'd like to question him about his accident. There are too many things going on at the same time. Let's also find the girl who was pushed into the pool. She should be around. As far as I know, only men went on the fishing trip."

Bernard and Michael nodded and followed Bianca down the hallway toward the old staircase.

Chapter Eleven

In the meantime, the men who had signed up for the deep-sea fishing trip, including Ryan Goslan, Samantha's ex-boyfriend, and Patrick Smith, had arrived at the Key West marina. They boarded their private charter boat, a Regulator 34 high performance center console boat, designed and engineered for the serious fisherman.

Despite the terrible events last night and this morning, the men were excited and in a good mood and trying not to think of Samantha Berg. The temperature was a balmy eighty degrees. The sun had burned off some clouds and was already standing high in the sky. The atmosphere in the busy harbor was rustling and bustling. Various scuba boats, some other deep-sea fishing boats, catamarans, and private boats were all getting ready to depart for their day trips. The calm aquamarine ocean glistened in the sun. A pod of silvery dolphins jumped out of the water in the distance, a pelican landed on a wooden pole on the dock. The first mate passed out cups of fresh coffee, cut pieces of fruit and bagels with cream cheese as the captain got the boat ready for departure. Soon, everyone was seated as the boat slowly chugged through the no-wake zone.

"Good morning, gentlemen, and welcome aboard Marlin Charter's best fishing boat, the *Pilar*. I'm Captain Bill Meyers," said the captain through the intercom system. He had accelerated and was now driving full throttle ahead. One of the men's baseball caps flew off his head and into the water. "Hang onto your hats, men," the captain laughed as he slowed down and circled around. His first mate plucked the hat out of the water with a long pole and handed it back to its owner.

He continued, "Yes, our boat is named after Hemingway's fishing boat *Pilar*, because that's the experience we're trying to give you. We'll be searching for big marlin and tuna. This is going to take us a few miles out into the Atlantic Gulf Stream, so please bear with us and enjoy the eighty minutes we'll be cruising out into deeper waters. I'll be pointing out special things to you, but please don't hesitate to ask if you see something and have questions."

The men sat and enjoyed the bumpy ride across the waves. The wind whipped their hair out of their faces, and some of them reapplied their sunscreen as they felt the sun burn their skin. After seventy minutes, the boat passed Fort Jefferson. The water still looked quite shallow, but Captain Bill announced, "We'll be reaching our destination and deeper water very soon. For now, enjoy the views of Fort Jefferson, a massive but unfinished coastal fortress. It is the largest brick masonry structure in the Americas and was made with over sixteen million bricks. The building covers sixteen acres. Among United States forts, only Fort Monroe in Virginia and Fort Adams in Rhode Island are larger. The fort is located on Garden Key in the lower Florida Keys within Dry Tortugas National Park, sixty-eight miles west of Key West."

The men, who had started drinking again, stopped joking for a while and listened to the captain. "If you ever get a chance to come back, snorkeling is magnificent here. You can also get here by seaplane. It's a splurge but much faster."

They left Fort Jefferson behind them and came to deeper dark blue water. The big game-fishing rods and reels were fastened to the boat's downrigger. Soon they started trolling, hoping they'd tempt a marlin to take their bait. After there was no activity for a while and they had almost given up, one of the men shouted, "Marlin!" A white marlin known for putting up a hard fight, had struck. The whole boat erupted in bustling activity, and the first mate helped Ryan pull his rod to the fighting chair and strapped him in. The men took turns fighting and reeling it closer to the boat as the marlin jumped out of the water and shook his head violently. It was only about six feet long, but it put up a fight for about two hours. Then the captain insisted on letting it go, which was one of the conditions of this fishing trip. Disappointed, the men took a few pictures with the marlin in the background before they cut it loose.

"Sorry, guys", said Captain Bill. "Those are the rules. You should be aware that blue marlins are listed as vulnerable to extinction and that the US is limited to a total recreational catch of two hundred and fifty combined blue marlin, white marlin and roundscale spearfish per year."

The men looked at each other. They were a bit tipsy again and disappointed, but they understood. They wouldn't have been able to eat that much marlin here anyway during their short stay, and they had made memories that would last a lifetime.

Captain Bill turned the boat around and put it in full throttle to start the drive back to Key West. Suddenly, there was a big splash that almost couldn't be heard due to the loud motor, but some of the men yelled, "Man overboard!" and got the captain's attention.

Captain Bill looked over his shoulder, stopped the boat, and carefully and slowly maneuvered back to the spot where Ryan, who had resurfaced after being catapulted into the ocean, was treading water, still coughing, and choking. The first mate grabbed a life preserver and carefully threw it next to Ryan. Ryan grabbed it and pulled it over his head and under his arms as he quickly swam over to the boat. Several men bent down to pull him out of the water. He just stood there for a second, taking a few deep breaths, then he looked up and yelled, "Someone pushed me!"

Chapter Twelve

Kelly was sitting by the water, her legs hanging down from the dock, still moping about the entire situation. She didn't know what was worse: possibly getting roofied and not being able to prove it unless she went to the police and had bloodwork done, waking up naked next to her boss this morning, finding a dead body right afterward, or quitting her secure job with great benefits and possibly heading into unemployment and homelessness. She never took a break because she usually enjoyed her job so much, but today she needed one.

The shuttle boat chugged up through the crystal-clear water with the guests returning from their deep-sea fishing trip. It had been a great day, again with lots of beer, Cuban rum and Mai Tais. Everyone was in a good mood except Ryan, who was still upset and convinced that someone had pushed him into the water, trying to kill him. As soon as Ryan discovered Kelly, he complained to her.

"Are the police still here? I want to report that someone pushed me off the fishing boat. Eighty miles out in the ocean. I don't think these incidents are a coincidence anymore."

Kelly stood up and smoothed her dress. She looked at him, truly concerned. "Are you okay?"

"I'm okay, but I'm really upset now. How is Ken doing, by the way? I want to talk to him."

Kelly realized that she hadn't wasted another thought on Ken who had surgery this morning and she felt even more awful. It had been such an eventful day.

"I'm sorry, the last time I called he was still in surgery. Let's go and see Charles together, and we can ask him if he's heard anything. You can also wait for the police in his office."

Ryan nodded and followed her into the building.

As Kelly walked through the lobby followed by Ryan, she ran into Gilda again and had to do a double take. Hadn't Gilda been here this morning and left hours ago? Little did Kelly know that Gilda was here out of curiosity and because she wanted to help with the case. Her "sleuth radar" had gone off, and she *had* to be here and watch what was going on. Gilda became a little obsessed once she set her mind to something. She had even already been upstairs in Samantha's room to check whether the broken pots could be cleaned up after she heard about them. Of course, they had to stay untouched, as evidence, and she was sent away.

Kelly and Ryan ran into the two police officers who were walking down the hallway coming from Charles' office.

"Can I talk to you?" asked Ryan without greeting them. "I think I might have some new information on the case."

"And you are who?" asked Bianca.

"Ryan Goslan. I belong to the VT Tech group."

Michael looked at Kelly. "Is there anywhere we can speak with him in private?" Kelly nodded. They were almost in front of the conference room. "I'll ask the front desk for the master key. Just a second."

She turned around, walked back down the hallway, and stepped up to the front desk to ask Claire for the master key. Gilda was there again! She stood next to Claire, pretending to be busy, pulling some dead flowers out of a big bouquet as they chit-chatted about the case and the group from Silicon Valley. Kelly gave her another double take and decided to have a word with her as soon as she had opened the conference room.

Gilda looked back at Kelly with a blank stare and decided she might have overstayed her welcome now and it was time to leave.

Kelly opened the door leading to the conference room for Police Officers Michael and Bianca as well as Ryan who were all standing there, waiting for her with serious faces.

"Please, sit down," said Michael to Ryan, pointing at the big round table in the middle of the conference room. "What's going on?"

"I just went on the deep-sea fishing trip, and someone pushed me off the boat as it was doing about thirty miles per hour. I could've been killed. That's not a coincidence."

Michael and Bianca looked at each other, taking in this news.

"I don't think I'm going on the dive trip tomorrow. Someone might slash my air hose… And I don't think it's a coincidence that my colleague fell down the stairs last night either."

The two officers nodded and waited for him to continue talking.

"I don't know if this has anything to do with it, but I dated Samantha a while ago, and I've been dating Lillian for a few weeks. Those two hated each other, and Lillian is extremely jealous. Samantha wasn't over us yet and was also extremely jealous and had been flirting with me non-stop, which Lillian wasn't too happy about."

"But Ms. Dumas wasn't on the fishing boat with you. So, who do you think pushed you?" asked Bianca.

"I don't know. Maybe she hired someone."

The two officers nodded as they took notes. That was a good start—they needed to interview Lillian and check her alibi as soon as possible.

Kelly walked back to the front desk to have a little talk with Gilda about her strange hours and being back at the hotel although she had already been here this morning. Gilda was gone though.

"Claire, do you know where Gilda went?" asked Kelly.

"No, she said she still has more work in the administration tract. But I'd think you would've run into her."

Gilda was tenacious. She had snuck back into the administrative hallway but quickly hid in the restroom as Kelly walked by. Now she stepped into Charles' office, pretending she was checking on the bouquet on the coffee table. He wasn't there. She briefly glanced at the paperwork on the desk and quickly read Kelly's resignation letter. She was impressed that Kelly was following through and really quitting her job. Then she noticed an adjoining door to the conference room, that was slightly ajar. Gilda held her ear up to it.

"How is my colleague in the hospital doing? Have you heard anything yet?"

"He's doing fine, should be released tomorrow. But he will have to be in a wheelchair for a while."

"He thinks he was pushed too. I have a theory, but I'm not sure if it makes sense because it would be way too obvious who the perpetrator is."

Michael and Bianca were all ears. So were Gilda and Kelly, who was just stepping into Charles' office. She gave Gilda a dirty look but realized that something very important was being said.

"At the end of the year, the executive who had the highest sales gets a bonus of *one hundred thousand dollars*. Lillian, Samantha, Ken and I are currently the top four. Doesn't that seem to be a bit of a coincidence? What if someone is trying to eliminate all of us to be number one?"

Michael and Bianca nodded. It would almost be

too obvious, but it was certainly a possibility.

"Is there a list of the top executives somewhere?" asked Michael.

"Yes, the top ten are listed on the homepage of the company's website which constantly changes. But the top ten are the group that's currently here."

"What's the website?"

"Www.vttech.com."

"What does VT stand for?"

"Victor Thomas, the founder."

"Do you know who number five is?" asked Bianca Ryan.

"It fluctuates depending on daily sales. Our sales don't stop while we're on vacation. But five and six are currently Conor Mitchum and Alex Barrios."

"Thanks for all this info," said Bianca and wrote down the two names. "Unfortunately, we need to ask you this routine question, just to confirm: So, you never left Ms. Dumas' room the night of Ms. Berg's death, and Ms. Dumas can confirm that you were with her?"

"I went back to my room at some point in the morning. I had to send out some work emails before I was going to be away from my laptop all day during the deep-sea fishing trip. That was probably around five thirty a.m."

"And Ms. Dumas was asleep?"

"Yes."

So, Ms. Dumas had been asleep and couldn't really confirm whether Ryan Goslan was in her room or not....

Chapter Thirteen

Gilda, what are you doing here?" whispered Kelly. She tried to be quiet so the police officers in the room next door wouldn't hear her. "You can't just hang out in Charles' office and eavesdrop on confidential conversations. What are you doing back here anyway? You were already here this morning."

Gilda came up with a quick excuse. "I think I was so shocked about what happened that I forgot some of my tools and had to come back to get them." Kelly just looked at her. She didn't believe that. If that was the case, she would have grabbed her tools and been out of there instead of lingering around and pretending to work – or she could've picked them up tomorrow.

"Well, let's get out of here before Charles comes back and finds us."

They stepped out of the office just as Michael and Bianca were stepping into the hallway. Bianca recognized Gilda and greeted her. "Hey Gilda, long time no see! I haven't seen you since you helped us with the case of the Cuban boy who was dealing drugs. What brings you out here?"

Of course, Gilda didn't want to admit that she was curious about the homicide. "Buenos dias, Bianca… Señor Brinkmann," she exclaimed, nodding at them both, to win some time. "Ummm, I take care of the flowers. I come out here on a regular basis."

Kelly looked at Gilda from the side. So, Officer Sanchez knew her, and she had helped the police previously? Was Gilda secretly a private detective or something? She had to get to the bottom of this.

Kelly checked the time on her smart phone. It was four p.m. but felt like ten. Today had been terribly long and tiring. Thank goodness it was time to go now, and she hadn't run into Charles again. She'd deal with him tomorrow. Gilda accompanied her back to her desk and from there they walked together to the boat shuttle.

The shuttle chugged along in the late afternoon sun. Kelly and Gilda sat in the bow under a yellow bimini top, looking toward the mainland with a row of hotels and shops, palm trees, tall hibiscus shrubs, and plumerias. A tropical paradise that Kelly tried to appreciate every day after growing up with the long winters in upstate New York.

"My husband worked for the police in Cuba, and I had planned on going to a police academy too before my family escaped from the communist regime in Cuba, moved here, and I had kids," explained Gilda. "I've always been interested in solving mysteries. One time I was able to help Bianca and Officer Brinkmann with a drug deal in my neighborhood. It really gave me a thrill, and they were very thankful." She added,

"Of course, the police in Cuba were very corrupt, and my husband was an exception. That's one of the reasons he had to leave."

Kelly looked at her. She had never thought about where Gilda came from and under what circumstances she had moved here and felt shallow for never asking.

"How old were you when you came here?"

"I had just graduated from high school and was about to go to police academy, but then I couldn't. We couldn't afford it here. So, I got married and had kids and started the flower business when my husband died. I love it and don't regret it."

"You certainly have a green thumb and an eye for flower arrangements," replied Kelly. "I'm sorry, I didn't even know your husband passed away."

"Don't worry, you couldn't. It's been over ten years."

"Do you have kids?"

"Yes, a son, Ricky, and a daughter, Sarah. But they're already out of the house. Ricky is a musician and goes to UCF in Orlando, and Sarah goes to UNF in Jacksonville with a full scholarship."

"Wow, sounds like you're very proud of them."

"Yes, they both do great. Ricky is a senior majoring in jazz studies and already has a lot of gigs on the side. Sometimes even here in Key West. He plays the saxophone. And Sarah is going to nursing school."

Kelly nodded. The boat pulled up to the dock and the first mate fastened the ropes in the front and back to the cleats. Kelly and Gilda had to wait a second until the coast was clear to get off the boat, and the first mate helped them climb out.

"Which way are you going?" asked Gilda as Kelly unlocked her bike. It seemed that she'd love to continue the conversation. Even though Kelly was tired and wanted to go home, she felt bad that she had never shown any interest in Gilda and said, "I live on Whitehead, but I know that place right over there has really good tapas." She was suddenly starving and realized she hadn't eaten all day. She pointed straight ahead at the little tapas bar. "Do you want to go and have a beer or so and some tapas?"

Gilda, who was a social butterfly and often became quite lonely since her kids had both moved out, was excited and nodded. "I'd love that! That place is actually very good, and I could use a drink. It's almost five o' clock!"

"I'll just leave my bike here then," Kelly said. They both walked across the street and entered the little hole-in-the-wall bar. To Kelly's surprise, the employees knew Gilda and greeted her like a long-lost friend.

"Gilda! Como estas!" the owner said, coming around the bar to kiss Gilda on both cheeks.

"Muy bien, gracias."

They both started talking so fast in Spanish that Kelly was absolutely lost with her two years of high school Spanish.

"I'm so sorry." Gilda finally remembered Kelly and interrupted her vivid conversation. "Yolanda, this is my coworker Kelly from the Casa Bella. She's the concierge there."

"Hola, Kelly, I've seen you here before."

She smiled.

Kelly smiled back. "Yes, I love this place. Nice to meet you."

They ordered some beers and tapas and, since they were just really getting to know each other, they could have talked for hours. Kelly told her about the situation with Charles, quitting her job and then subsequently losing her apartment. Housing in Key West was astronomical. Most people had to live in the upper Keys, which were a bit less expensive, and had long commutes to and from work.

"Oy, that's not good," said Gilda. Without hesitation, she offered. "I'm very proud of you that you followed through and quit though. You shouldn't have to deal with a boss like that. You know, I have two empty rooms in my house since my kids moved out. You can stay with me. Even if it's until you find something else."

Kelly felt that was too much to ask, but she could also tell that Gilda meant it and was probably lonely.

"Thanks, Gilda, but I really feel like I'd be imposing. Can I get back to you if I need to?

"Yes, of course. Just think about it. It's an option. My house is older but quite spacey. And I have a very big yard. We won't drive each other crazy."

"Thank you. I really appreciate it and might really have to accept your generous offer."

They got the check and stepped out into the balmy evening. It was already getting dark, and the cicadas were chorusing. Up the road at Mallory Square, the "Sunset Celebration" was taking place. Hundreds of tourists had gathered to watch the sunset, with arts and crafts exhibitors, street performers, and food trucks offering their services. From afar, they saw a fire-eater performing, surrounded by a group of people. Kelly walked across the street to get her bike. Gilda followed her to get her flower cart. Suddenly, they both saw something black crawling underneath the bike. They took a closer look. It was a helpless little kitten, not more than a few weeks old!

Chapter Fourteen

Kelly carefully picked up the kitten. It seemed like it must've just opened its eyes, which were the brightest light blue.

"Wow, look at its eyes," said Kelly to Gilda.

"All kittens have blue eyes. They change when they're about six weeks old, so this poor thing is under six weeks. It looks like a little bat, doesn't it, with those big ears and the black face? And look," Gilda pointed at the kitten's belly which had a white diamond on it, another black diamond inside that, and a white neck. "It's a tuxedo cat, it looks like it's wearing a vest."

Kelly cringed as Gilda took the kitten out of her hands quite ungently by the scruff of its neck. She looked like she had experience with kittens though and did a quick examination. The kitten, which was female, had all its limbs and looked quite good besides the fact that it was very young and had been separated from its mother. Gilda continued. "We should check if its mother or any other kittens are around," said Gilda as she looked around under some hibiscus shrubs. No mother cat or other kittens were to be found. It looked like they were stuck with the kitten, and Kelly panicked a little because she had no idea what to do. But Gilda did.

"We should call the humane society first." She looked at her phone. "But they might be closed already." She googled the number of the local humane society and called it, but there was no answer, just an answering machine. "I guess we're stuck with the kitty, at least for tonight," Gilda said and looked at her again. "What should we call her?" Kelly looked at her nervously. As soon as they named the kitten, they'd be attached and not want to give her away. But Gilda seemed to know what she was doing.

"How about Zoë?" Kelly had just watched Cat Woman with Zoë Kravitz and thought it was a good match.

"Perfect!" Gilda exclaimed and looked at Kelly. "Listen, amiga. I know you must be terribly tired after last night. I'll be glad to take care of her for tonight. She needs a special kitten milk and needs to be fed with a bottle every two to three hours. It's not easy."

Kelly appreciated Gilda's offer, but she was eager to help. "What if I get the kitten milk and you get her home so that you don't have to carry her around or leave her alone?"

"That would be great. Walmart should have the kitten milk. It's called KMR, kitten milk replacement — or the Pet Supermarket on Roosevelt has it. It comes in cans or as a powder. I think they're open until nine. We also need some pet baby bottles and nipples. I'll text you my address, it's on this side of Flagler. Not far from here. About a ten-minute walk."

The kitten in Gilda's hand meowed loudly and pitifully. It was hungry.

"Okay, I see I need to get going," said Kelly. "I'll be as fast as possible."

"Text me if you can't find the KMR or nipples. I'll call around if we need to get them somewhere else. Maybe one of my friends has some."

Kelly nodded.

She got on her bike and pedaled toward North Roosevelt Boulevard, which was a more commercial shopping street heading out of Key West toward the Overseas Highway. Gilda headed home, carefully holding the kitten in one hand against her body and pulling her cart behind her with the other.

Daylight faded, a balmy breeze had come up, and the moon was rising in the sky. A few great white herons flew over Gilda toward the ocean, making their typical croaking squeals. Gilda looked down at the kitten and said quietly, "Boy, am I glad they didn't get you for dinner." Then she gently added, calling the kitten by her name, "Sweet little Zoë…"

Kelly's trip to Pet Supermarket was successful, and they had everything she needed including tiny bottles and nipples for kittens with little brushes to wash them. She checked out quickly and went back the way she had come. She had the GPS app on her phone on and followed Siri's instructions back to Gilda's house.

It was getting darker, and Kelly came to a neighborhood that she wasn't used to. Some of the streets showed a side of Key West that hadn't changed much in 100 years. Kelly rode through an area that Cuban cigar workers had once occupied. These simple Bahamas-style cottages were small and narrow shotgun houses, named like that because one could fire a shotgun in the front door and have the bullets exit the back door without hitting anything in between.

This was the more Latin as well as Asian neighborhood in Key West, also known as Midtown. She passed a house that had Latin music blasting out of the open windows and clothes drying on a line in the side yard. A baby in a swing cried on someone's front porch and some kids were running home. Darkness was their curfew. A big pit bull behind a picket fence started barking as Kelly passed, and she startled. He wagged his tail.

She took a left onto a small cul-de-sac at the edge of the neighborhood and came up to a house surrounded by a beautiful tropical garden and a forest of bamboo. She double-checked the house number on the mailbox. This was Gilda's property. Kelly hesitated. At first, it seemed a bit scary, because it was so overgrown and dark, but then she stepped past the bamboo and came up to an opening in the "jungle" with a big water fountain and little twinkling fairy lights hanging in the trees surrounding the fountain. A cozy two-story light pink conch house with illuminated windows and a little front porch filled with plant stands, a table, rocking chairs, and blooming orchids became visible to Kelly, and she felt right at home. She could tell that the person who lived here really loved her home and took great care of it. She climbed up five or six steps to the front door, couldn't find a doorbell and knocked.

Nobody answered. Kelly knocked again. She heard uplifting Latin music coming from inside the house. Just as she was about to knock again loudly, the door was opened with full force. A shirtless muscular young man in his early to mid-twenties, with short dark curly hair, beautiful dark brown eyes, full lips, and a chiseled chin opened the door. For a second they were both silent and just stared at each other. Kelly wondered if she was at the wrong house. She felt like her face was turning beet red.

"Oh, I'm sorry, I thought you were a buddy of mine," said the man. Even his voice was sexy.

Chapter Fifteen

Gilda came up behind him. "Ricky, my gosh, go put a shirt on. Sorry, Kelly, this is my son Ricky. He stopped by for a surprise gig in town and always needs to strut around, showing off his abs." Ricky and Gilda both grinned at each other.

Ricky replied with a chuckle, "Sorry, Ma, I was just working out and heard the knocking. I thought it was Alex."

Another young guy who also looked like he was in great shape stepped up behind Kelly. "There he is," said Ricky. "Hey, bro. Come on in." They both disappeared to the back of the house but not without giving Kelly another quick glance, who they obviously both found interesting.

Kelly quickly changed the subject to not stare as they walked away. "How's the kitty? I got everything. Here." She started unpacking the bag and placed the items on the kitchen counter tiled with pink '80s tile.

"What'd you get? The powder or the cans?" Gilda asked and stepped up to the counter.

"They only had the powder."

"That's okay because it ends up lasting longer and

being much cheaper. This will last us for about two weeks," said Gilda as she looked at the can and then unpacked the bottle and nipples. She washed them with dish soap and dried them off. Then she got out a measuring spoon and prepared a mixture of kitten food with water that she microwaved for a few seconds to warm it up to the perfect temperature. She then carefully poured it into the bottle's small opening with a small funnel, holding it over the sink in case she spilled something. Two cats had followed her into the kitchen and were rubbing up against her legs and checking Kelly out, but when Kelly tried to pet them, they jumped away.

"These are two former strays, they're still a little shy with strangers. This is Buzzie," she said pointing at the big orange tabby, "and this is Picasso." She pointed at the beautiful calico that absolutely looked like out of a Picasso painting with its geometric looking markings. "And there are three more on the screened porch in the back."

Kelly added up in her head. That made five cats already. "Yes," said Gilda reading her mind and grinning. "You could call me a crazy cat lady. I foster even more from time to time," she continued. "That's why little Zoë is in the bathroom right now. I don't know how the other cats will react to her, and we need her confined so that we don't lose her crawling around somewhere in the house or someone stepping on her."

Kelly nodded and followed her to the bathroom where Gilda had already put the tiny kitten in a little crate with a heating pad. A feeding station was set up on the counter next to the sink with an old puppy pad that Gilda had found in her garage and a roll of paper towels. She opened the crate and carefully got the tiny kitten out that had hidden under the soft blanket Gilda had put in there. It immediately started meowing loudly.

"Let me show you how this works," said Gilda as she set the kitten down on the counter. She held it with her left hand, and with her right she held the bottle up in front of the kitten's face so that the tip of the bottle was pointing down and the milk was slowly dripping out. The kitten eagerly tried to take the nipple in its mouth but had a hard time keeping it in its tiny mouth and started biting it. "It has teeth, meaning it's at least three or four weeks old," stated Gilda. "Thank goodness, the older, the better her survival chances are."

Finally, the kitten latched on to the nipple and suckled about half an ounce of the kitten replacement milk.

"So, now to the worst part," said Gilda as she started gently massaging the area around the kitten's butt. "With a kitten this young, we need to massage its bottom. The mother usually licks that area, stimulating the kitten to poop and pee... She might be old enough already to do it on her own, but I'm not sure."

"Oh, wow," said Kelly. She was flabbergasted. How was someone who found a kitten like this supposed to know that had to be done?

Gilda showed her the tiny yellow pee stain on the

puppy pad, handed her the kitten and washed her hands.

"So, this needs to be done about every three hours," Gilda said and set the timer app on her phone.

Kelly had expected something like that but was in shock. How were they going to keep up with that?

"We can try calling the humane society in the morning. There's also a Facebook page, "Keys Kitten Rescue." We can post on that page and see if anyone is willing to take her. I've dealt with them before, they're very helpful."

Kelly already felt attached to the kitten and made a face. However, with her work schedule she really wouldn't be able to keep up with feeding her every few hours— but, hey! She wouldn't have a work schedule soon. She was about to be unemployed! And homeless…

"Gilda, about the room you said I might be able to rent…"

Gilda nodded and put the kitten back in the crate who seemed ready to go back. "Follow me," she said as she walked down a short hallway and up a creaky old wooden staircase to her daughter's currently unused room. She turned the light on, and a typical teenage girl's room became visible, with lots of flowery pillows and girly details and little pictures of heartthrob popstars and actors. "Of course, it's dark right now, but it's a really nice sunny room, facing out to the backyard." Some palm fronds scraped against the windows, and Kelly could hear the bamboo canes outside swaying in the wind, clicking and clacking against each other. It sounded like relaxing music. "I can rent it to you for a couple hundred dollars, really to cover the utilities, until you're back on your feet. Let me show you the bathroom."

Kelly, in panic mode, said, "I don't even have to see the bathroom, it's a perfect solution for now and that way we can take turns taking care of Zoë. Will you be able to take care of her tonight? That way I can go home and pack a few things and move in slowly over the next few days." Gilda was thrilled to have a roommate. "Sure. And I was going to offer to take care of Zoë anyhow. I didn't expect you to be available for something like that with your job."

"Well, it looks like I'll be unemployed in a few days and have all the time in the world," replied Kelly, frowning.

In this instance, Ricky and his friend Alex came stomping up the old wooden stairs. Kelly realized that he'd also be her roommate when he was in Key West and she'd probably be sharing a bathroom with him…a bit awkward, but as she took another look at him, now with a shirt on, she didn't think she'd mind that too much…

Chapter Sixteen

Kelly stepped out of the pretty cottage and took one last look around as she walked through the overgrown yard and unlocked her bike that she had chained to the white picket fence. A dog barked somewhere in the distance, and an owl hooted up in the bamboo. The moon was up in the clear sky and there was a slight breeze that made Kelly's dress billow in the wind. Another heavy downpour in the evening had lowered the humidity and made the sub-tropical heat bearable again. Sometimes in the summer, it was so hot and humid that people broke out in a sweat and their glasses fogged up as soon as they stepped outside. But tonight, Kelly could breathe, and it felt nice. Maybe fall was in the air. It was almost mid-September, and time to cool down a little, but it was still hurricane season. Kelly liked this neighborhood. It was in the middle of town but seemed quiet and not too busy, at least in this cul-de-sac. Before jumping onto her bike, she pushed it a little and walked past the houses and yards of Gilda's neighbors. They weren't as upscale as the houses on Whitehead but quaint little colorful cottages with pretty, overgrown yards. Kelly walked up to White Street, then jumped on her bike and rode through the dark streets of Key West. It was barely a five-minute ride home. She took a left onto Truman and went all the way down to Whitehead. The streets were still full of tourists walking around, shopping, and going out to dinner. Key West was always busy with a bustling atmosphere.

Kelly got off her bike, walked past the main building up to the garden house, and ran into Max, who was sitting on the little balcony in front of his downstairs apartment, having a beer after work. Kelly was tired and resented a tiny little bit that she constantly ran into people she knew everywhere, but of course she stopped and chit-chatted with him.

"Hey, Max! You're not gonna believe what Gilda and I just found. A three- or four-week-old kitten. Right at the boat shuttle."

"Oh, wow, do you have any pictures?"

She got out her phone and pulled up the photos and videos she had taken. "Here you go." She showed him a short video of the kitten in Gilda's hands, meowing pitifully.

"Wow, I love tuxedo cats," said Max. "It's adorable. So, Gilda's taking care of it?"

"Yeah, it's more practical right now." She paused for a second. Should she already spread the news or not? "And by the way I quit my job. So, I'm gonna need to move out of here, and she offered me to stay at her house."

"Oh, no, you've got to be kidding me." He was

really upset. "I can't lose you as my neighbor."

Kelly looked at Max. For the first time, she realized that he might have feelings for her, and she thought to herself, *how stupid am I, to not notice that earlier?* What an awkward situation. She saw him looking at her and quickly looking away when she looked back at him. She tried to get out of talking to him for tonight and said, "I'm really tired, I've really got to..." But Max had already opened a bottle of beer for her and pulled his second chair up, their usual ritual. She sat down, and he handed her the beer. There was an awkward silence as they sat there, staring into the dark.

"I can't stay, Max, after what happened between me and Charles the other night. I woke up in his bed, naked. I'm not a homewrecker. He's married and has three kids."

Max was shocked. He knew that Kelly and Charles had left the banquet together but not that she had slept in his room. He immediately changed his mind and supported her decision. She *had to* get away from the hotel and Charles, even if he, Max, wouldn't see her as often. "Maybe that's a good decision," he said. "But what are you gonna do for work?"

"Well, there are lots of hotels in Key West and if all else fails, I'll start freelancing as a concierge. Gilda knows someone who does that and said she has a lot of work. The sad thing is that I won't be able to stay here anymore. I love this apartment."

Max nodded and took a leap of faith. "Well, you know my apartment is a little bigger than yours. I have the spare room. You can stay with me for a while if you want."

He paused, took a sip of beer, and looked at her from the side, insecure. "As a friend, I mean," he added, blushing.

Kelly was glad she had the kitten as an excuse. Max was a good friend and it was a generous offer, but not if there were feelings involved. "Thanks, Max, but you know, with the kitten, we're kind of sharing the responsibility…"

"Well, if things don't work out, you know you always have a room here."

"Thanks, Max!" She held up her beer bottle to clink his, and they both took another swig.

Something came to Kelly's mind. "Max, didn't you tell me that you used to work for a tech company in Silicon Valley?"

Max took another big swig of his beer before he answered.

"Yup. It was the same one those guys work for, VT Tech."

"Wow, what a coincidence!" replied Kelly.

"Not really. Because I was sent here on one of those fully paid trips too, and that's how I fell in love with Key West. I was among the top ten associates one year. They've always had a relationship with the Casa Bella. The owners' son is one of the CEOs of VT Tech. But let me tell you something, they have bad business practices. Fifty percent of the employees, including me, get burn-out syndrome from the chronic stress and constant pressure to be among the best. I almost had a heart attack, imagine that, at my age, and had to quit. I couldn't take the constant pressure any longer and decided to turn my hobby, cooking, into my new career. I had gone to culinary school before working at VT Tech but was also always a computer Wiz. And even though running a kitchen is stressful, it's nothing compared to working for that company." He paused for a second, grabbed another beer from a small cooler next to his chair, and opened it.

Kelly listened, shocked. She had never seen Max so worked up and angry. Usually, he was rather laid back and quiet.

Max continued his angry tirade. Kelly just listened, shocked. "In the short time I worked there, I saw several lives being destroyed. Everyone who wasn't among the top ten was labeled a loser. Lots of people ended up having depression or getting sick with something else, heart attacks, skin issues, caused by stress. Ryan Goslan was already at the company when I worked there. He's quite the prick and changes his girlfriends like his underwear. He's among the top ten on a regular basis though, maybe even the top five."

Suddenly, Kelly couldn't help but wonder whether Max had something to do with all the accidents the VT Tech group was having. Was he capable of something like that, even murder?

Chapter Seventeen

Bianca Sanchez sat there staring at her phone, flabbergasted and stressed. Her chief, who was never in the office this early, had just read her the riot act about how urgently this case had to be solved and hung up on her quite rudely. She took another sip of her already-cold black coffee and called her colleague Michael on speed dial.

He was still at home finishing breakfast. He looked at the clock as he stuck his last piece of toast into his mouth and answered the phone.

"Hey, Bianca! What's going on this early? It's only six forty-five."

"I couldn't sleep, and Chief Cameron just called and reprimanded me about the case. The tech group is leaving on Wednesday, and we have no evidence to keep them from departing Key West. We need to solve this case stat before they're all scattered about in California."

"Oh, no," replied Michael. His blood pressure went up immediately. It was never good when the chief started getting impatient. He could be very intimidating.

"Can you meet me at the Casa Bella boat shuttle at seven instead of the office? That's when the shuttle departs. We can have a coffee there, wait in the breakfast room, and question the group members. I want to question the guy who broke his leg and had surgery, I think that's Ken Miller, and Ryan Goslan one more time. And, of course, Lillian Dumas. She and Goslan are currently our main suspects."

"Yes, I'll drive right over there. See you in a few."

The two officers arrived simultaneously at the boat dock, parked their cars, and jumped into the empty shuttle that was about to depart for Little Orchid Island.

Ken Miller was sitting in the Casa Bella breakfast room in a wheelchair with a long metal contraption holding up his injured leg, having a breakfast for kings as well as a tall bloody Mary with a few skewers of shrimp and blue-cheese-filled olives.

"I might as well get my money's worth in food since there's nothing else left for me to do," he said grinning and pointing at his elevated leg after the officers had greeted him and introduced themselves.

"We're so sorry about your leg," said Bianca. "Does it hurt badly?"

"It's okay, it only hurts if I move around too much. Trust me, that the hospital gave me plenty of pain medication. The boat shuttle is a bit of a pain with the wheelchair, so I'm kind of stuck on the island unless some of my buddies take me into town. Oh, and the elevator here is on the small side, but I don't want to bore you with details about my leg."

"Would you mind if we joined you and asked you a few questions?" asked Bianca.

"No, go ahead," he replied, upbeat. "I'm happy about the company." He laughed and added, "And I'm feeling like James Stewart in 'Rear Window', just sitting around, watching everyone and hearing all the gossip all day. Most of my buddies probably won't wake up until later, and some of them already left on a scuba diving trip."

Bianca and Michael exchanged quick glances. A diving accident could easily be fatal...

Ken noticed their look. "Yeah, I was thinking the same thing. I wouldn't go diving with all these accidents that have been happening. Ryan wasn't going to go either but ended up changing his mind. I think he was afraid to come across as a coward. His girlfriend Lillian is big into diving and really wanted to go."

So, those two wouldn't be back until late in the afternoon or early evening.

A female server walked up and offered Bianca and Michael coffee.

"Are you two having breakfast?" she asked. They both hesitated. The Casa Bella was known to be outrageously expensive, and police officers didn't make that much money, but in that instance, Charles walked up and handed them a few breakfast vouchers.

"We don't want our friends and helpers to go hungry," he said with a smile, then asked, "Will you come see me in my office when you're done here? If I'm not there, just ask the front desk. They'll know where I am."

They nodded, thanked him, and asked Ken whether he needed anything before they walked over to the impressive buffet. A few minutes later, they returned with plates filled with made-to-order omelettes, bacon, cheese, cut fruit and fresh croissants.

"Sorry about that," said Bianca apologetically as she cut a piece of her omelette. "We might as well take advantage. It's going to be a long day if your colleagues aren't coming back until later in the afternoon from their dive trip."

Ken nodded. "Sure, no problem. Bon appetit."

"So, what do you think about this entire situation? Do you think it's a coincidence or that someone is attacking you and your colleagues?"

"I think someone pushed me. There's no way I would have stumbled over something or fallen down the stairs like that."

"We did hear that there was some heavy drinking at the bar in the late afternoon. May we ask how many drinks you had?"

He scowled a bit, insulted.

"I had two or three Mai Tais, but that's not unusual for me. Work hard, play hard is my motto. I'm on vacation."

They both nodded and glanced at his bloody Mary. Two or three Mai Tais could have impaired his focus and coordination. Maybe two or three had even been three or four. And today he was already drinking at seven a.m., probably on top of some heavy-duty medication.

"And what do you think about your colleague Lillian falling into the pool? Do you think she was also pushed?"

He thought for a second. "Honestly, I'm not sure. She did seem a bit out of it that afternoon. And the pool is close to the bar, and we were a big group there. I think that's a whole different situation. She could've just stepped back and fallen into the pool."

"Did you know that Ryan and Samantha were an item before he got together with Lillian?"

"Yeah, everyone knows that Ryan is quite the ladies' man. I was wondering if Lillian pushed Samantha off the balcony out of jealousy. Maybe Samantha was trying to get him back. She was quite flirtatious with him at the pool after Lillian had fallen in and left. But would you kill someone because of that?"

"Maybe they had an argument, and it was an accident," replied Bianca.

Ken nodded. "They used to be best friends, so it's an awkward situation. Especially to be on vacation together."

"Ryan told us that you four are the four 'highest ranking' employees in your company. Isn't that a bit much of a coincidence?" Michael googled the company's website and looked at the top ten employees of the year listed on the homepage. "So, Conor Mitchum is number five. I wonder if he's the next one to have an accident…"

"I think he's on the dive trip too. We'd better all keep an eye on him..." said Ken, sucking vigorously on his bloody Mary's straw.

They weren't going anywhere with this conversation, and since they were done with breakfast, Bianca and Michael thanked Ken, left a few dollar bills as a tip on the table with two of the vouchers, and stepped out of the dining room and into the lobby. They stood there for a second. They were both suddenly very nervous about the dive trip.

"We should've stopped the dive trip," said Bianca. "Or one of us should have gone undercover."

Michael nodded. But it was too late now. They headed toward Charles' office who pleaded them to find the perpetrator.

"I'm afraid heads are going to roll if we can't solve this case soon," Charles said desperately. "The owners are not too happy, and people are canceling their reservations and leaving early."

"We're doing our best," replied Officer Sanchez. She and Officer Brinkmann were feeling the pressure from all sides.

Chapter Eighteen

Meanwhile, the dive boat with five of the VT Tech colleagues, including Ryan and Lillian, as well as some other divers, had arrived at the reef and anchored. Some of the divers had already been preparing and putting on their equipment, but Ryan, Lillian, and a few others had been chatting and were still working on getting their dive equipment assembled. The air tanks were attached to the BCs, the regulator was screwed onto the valve, the low-pressure inflator hose was hooked up, then the air was turned on. They checked their pressure gauges, whether their octopus and their primary regulators were working, and fastened the hoses to their vests. The BCs were checked to ensure they were inflating and deflating properly, and then everyone grabbed their masks and fins and got ready to jump into the water.

"Ladies and gentlemen, please make sure you always stay with your designated dive buddy," said the captain through the intercom system. "Always stay in the group, and follow our dive-master, Doug.

He will be pointing out special things he sees. This will be an easy shallow dive, and we won't be exceeding about forty-five feet. At the end of the dive, you will still have to do the five-to-six-minute safety stop to decompress, so please keep that in mind. You should all have about three thousand pounds of air, which will last you from thirty to forty-five minutes. Everyone, please check your gauges!" Everyone checked their pressure gauges and made a thumbs up sign. The captain continued, "You should have about five hundred psi left when you emerge from the water, so don't stay under too long. Don't forget, the more relaxed you are, the less air you'll use, so relax and enjoy the views. Now, enjoy your dive! Any more questions?"

Nobody answered. There was busy activity on board as the divers did a final check of their equipment and, one by one, jumped off the boat's stern into the crystal-clear water, holding their hands in front of their masks to not lose them as they hit the water's surface.

Ryan and Lillian were dive buddies. He followed her close by, checking out her shapely bottom and long tanned legs. They were the last two in the group and didn't pay much attention to the divemaster or the others since they were far ahead of them. They just did their own thing. Lillian pointed out an octopus floating along the bottom of the ocean and a moray eel disappearing in between some staghorn coral. A nurse shark came up slowly, and Lillian's eyes grew wide. She hid behind Ryan, but the nurse shark just ignored them and swam by. A big school of parrot fish swam up and they watched them, amazed as they started audibly chomping on the coral. It sounded funny.

Suddenly, Lillian grabbed her throat, and her eyes grew wide again. She quickly swam up to Ryan, who was distracted watching the parrot fish. She shook his arm and moved her flat hand across her throat in a slicing motion, indicating that her air supply was cut off. At first, he thought she was just kidding, but then he realized she was dead serious. He quickly located and grabbed his octopus, helped her remove her regulator, put the octopus into her mouth, and made sure she was breathing and —most importantly— calming down. The last thing she should do right now was shoot up to the surface. They had to slowly swim up to about twenty feet and decompress for five to six minutes. They checked their depth gauges, swam up a bit and just hung out for a while as Ryan kept an eye on his stopwatch, which he had set for five minutes. He tried her regulator and, indeed, he couldn't get any air through it either, even though the gauge showed that she still had fifteen hundred pounds. The regulator's gauge must have been broken, and the oxygen tank was empty! Finally, they were able to ascend and came up to the surface, taking their BCs out of their mouths.

Lillian was surprisingly calm, but Ryan was furious. "Gosh darn it, your regulator must be broken! It's showing half full, but that tank is totally empty! I'm going to give that dive shop a piece of my mind!"

Everyone at the hotel and the police already knew what had happened when the five divers returned, since Ryan had made a big stink at the dive shop and had already informed Officer Sanchez. She and Michael were waiting for him and Lillian in the lobby, accompanied by Charles when they entered the lobby with their other three colleagues.

"We are all gonna get killed here!" he yelled, as he saw Officers Sanchez and Brinkmann. "I don't know about my coworkers, but I'm out of here."

"Please stay, for the sake of solving this case. I assure you that we will fill this place with undercover agents who will be watching you like hawks."

Ryan hesitated and looked at Lillian.

"We really need your cooperation," pleaded Bianca again.

"Are you okay?" asked Ryan, looking at Lillian with a worried expression on his face.

"I'll stay," said Lillian. "But I'll lie by the pool and go shopping the rest of the time. Those are two quite safe activities." She grinned, knowing that her action-packed boyfriend had other things in mind.

He grinned at her and nodded, then looked at Bianca. "If Lillian stays, I'll stay too. After all, I need to keep an eye on her."

Chapter Nineteen

Just as Kelly settled down at her desk the next morning to do some research for a guest who wanted to do several excursions with his family in the next few days, Charles stepped up to her desk.

"May I?" he asked and sat down in the chair in front of Kelly without waiting for a reply. "I don't accept your resignation, Kelly. Don't you think we can work things out?" He stared at her with his piercing blue eyes, but they didn't have the same effect on her anymore after seeing his wife and kids yesterday. She was done. With him and this job. "My decision is final," she replied. "I have five vacation days left, so I'll work until next Wednesday, Thursday and Friday being my two days off. That's also the day the VT Tech group leaves, so you won't need me anymore after that."

"Please, Kelly, can't we talk about this? You know the hotel needs you. And I do too."

"I'd say, your wife and three kids need you even more," she snapped at him. "I don't know what happened the other night, but I'm assuming someone put a roofie in my drink. I won't report that to the police, but leaving will be my consequence. I can't let something like that happen again. I will not be drugged while I'm working. And I'm not a homewrecker."

Claire and her team behind the front desk, as well as some bellboys, heard Kelly's angry voice and looked up. Both Kelly and Charles noticed that people in the lobby were starting to look around because they heard their argument.

"Can't we take this to my office?"

"No, we're done here," replied Kelly.

The woman from the other day—this time in a different very pink Lilly Pulitzer dress, white sneakers, and a pink sports visor on her head—stepped up behind Charles. She looked like she'd just come from playing a tennis match.

Kelly looked past Charles and greeted her.

"Oh, hi, Mrs… McGaffy!" Kelly was proud to remember her name. She was good at remembering clients' names. "Is there anything I help you with?"

Charles had to accept the fact that he couldn't continue the conversation with a guest listening and begrudgingly disappeared into his office.

"Please call me Marilyn," Mrs. McGaffy replied, smiling, and sat down in the chair Charles had left empty. "Well, I was going to ask you about scuba diving trips, but I heard that there was an accident during a dive yesterday. Do you know any details?"

Kelly hesitated, but it wasn't a secret and had even been on the local news, thanks to Ryan's non-existent discretion. "Yes, we had a group out on a dive boat at the Western Sambos, one of the biggest reefs in the Keys, and one of the divers seemed to have a faulty gauge on her regulator. She ran out of air and had to breathe through her buddy's octopus."

"Oh, it was a woman? I'm sorry to hear that. But she's okay, I hope?"

"Yes, she's fine, and none of the dives here are really that deep. So, if you're still interested, I'll be glad to set you up. I'm sure this was just an isolated incident, and the dive shops will be checking their gear twice as well from now on."

"That's true, well, let me think about it. I only have a couple of days left, so I'm not sure if I really want to do it. Too many plans and too little time. I'm also interested in going to see the Turtle Hospital in Marathon. Do you have any info on that?"

The Turtle Hospital in Marathon was one of Kelly's favorite destinations. "Yes, it's really nice! Did you drive or fly here? Because if you drove, I'd recommend stopping there on your way back to Miami. It's an hour drive up the Keys toward Miami."

"Yes, I drove, so that would make sense. I'd also love to stop at the resort where the series "Bloodline" was filmed. Do they have any 'behind the scenes' tours?"

"There is not a 'behind the scenes' tour per se and The Moorings is an exclusive resort only for guests, but I know of a captain who takes people out on his boat and shows them some of the locations from the water. I highly recommend it."

Marilyn McGaffy suddenly saw someone in the restaurant and was distracted. She got up and said, "Thanks, Kelly, let me think about it. See you later!" she said in a singsong voice, then stood up and walked away.

Kelly took a deep breath and checked if the people at the front desk were still staring over. But their interest had disappeared when Charles left. She felt good that she had remained consistent and not let Charles talk her into staying just because he was lazy and didn't feel like finding a new concierge.

She wondered what the kitten and Gilda were doing. In that instance, Gilda stepped into the lobby, pulling her little wagon full of fresh flowers and tools behind her. Gilda was cheerful as usual as she walked up to Kelly to greet her, even though she had probably gotten up every three hours last night to feed the kitten.

"Gilda, how can you look so fresh after taking care of the kitten all night?" asked Kelly, smiling. "How is little Zoë?"

Without asking, Gilda sat down in the chair in front of Kelly's desk and started picking some dry flowers out of the bouquet on top of it and replacing them with fresh ones. "I never sleep anyhow — menopause. I have hot flashes all night," she said matter-of-factly. "Zoë's doing great. She drank more than I'd expected — and pooped a lot." She grinned. "I called the humane society, and they can't take her because she's too young. All their volunteers are busy too, so I guess we're stuck with her."

Kelly nodded. She didn't mind because the kitten was so adorable, and she already felt attached to her. "Well, I'll pack some clothes together after work and come to your house and help you tonight. We can take turns. Who's taking care of her now, or do you have to get back soon?"

"Ricky's done this before. I told him to feed her at nine-thirty. And then I need to be back at twelve-thirty. Every three hours is fine."

Kelly cringed. That was a tough schedule. But she had promised to help and was going to stick to it. It looked like Gilda was more flexible during the next few days, and she was going to have to step up at night.

Their conversation got interrupted by the sudden noise of someone running down the old wooden staircase. It was Lillian, followed by Ryan. She looked like she'd been crying. Lillian continued running through the lobby and then outside through the front door. Ryan called her, but he realized that everyone was watching the scene. He slowed down a little, nodded slightly at Kelly and Gilda, and walked out of the main entrance. Then he picked up the pace again and ran after Lillian, who was running toward the boat shuttle. The bellboys watched, bewildered, shaking their heads as he caught up with her and grabbed her arm. Kelly and Gilda could see a little through the big front picture windows and stretched their necks, trying to watch what was going on without seeming too nosy.

"Let go of me, you prick," yelled Lillian as she tried to pry his hand off her arm. "I wouldn't be surprised if you killed Samantha! Was I going to be next? During the dive?"

The captain of the boat shuttle, who had overheard Lillian's last sentence, walked up to check whether she needed help.

"Are you alright, ma'am?"

"Yes, I'm okay, thank you," she replied, breathing heavily. Ryan had let go of her arm and said, "Everything's okay, Captain, just seems we both woke up on the wrong side of the bed." He watched Lillian climb into the shuttle and said pleadingly, "Please, Lillian, let's talk about this."

She ignored him and looked out into the distance as she sat down by the railing, her jaw tightened, but her eyes filled up with tears again.

The boat departed with a short *honk* and chugged toward Key West. Ryan just stood there for a while, watching the vessel. Finally, he turned around and shuffled back to the hotel, losing a flip-flop, and cursing quietly.

Chapter Twenty

Ryan came back into the hotel. He walked through the lobby and upstairs with a hanging head. He looked like he had run out of his room without having a shower or being properly dressed. Both Kelly and Gilda looked at each other.

"Do you think it was him?" asked Gilda.

"Well, if Samantha wanted to get back together with him, he definitely has a motive," replied Kelly, "but Lillian could be the perpetrator too. If she wanted to get rid of Samantha."

Gilda nodded. "We should tell Officer Sanchez. And we should ask the shuttle captain if he heard anything else. And how Lillian acted on the boat." Her sleuth radar was back up with full force, and it seemed contagious. Kelly was really getting into it too, and her brain was churning with all the different possible suspects. Even Max might be one of them! Kelly told Gilda about her conversation with him last night and about Max's anger, which had totally taken her by surprise. "Oy," said Gilda, shaking her head. "This company sounds horrible, and everyone who works or worked there might be a suspect!"

Kelly nodded, and as she looked up, she saw Ken in his wheelchair and some other members of the group having breakfast in the restaurant. She looked through one of her drawers and found a small pad of breakfast vouchers. She knew this was overstepping her boundaries, but she tore a voucher off and pushed it over to Gilda with a sneaky grin.

"Gilda, why don't you go and have breakfast and see if you can listen to some of those conversations in there?"

Gilda looked at the voucher, beaming. Breakfast at the Casa Bella was not only known to be very expensive but also very exquisite, and she would've never been able to afford it.

Gilda thanked her, picked up the voucher, and walked into the dining room, where she pretended to stumble over Ken's wheelchair.

"Oh, I'm so sorry, I totally didn't see your wheelchair. Oh, wow, I hope I didn't hurt you, what did you do to your leg?" Within two minutes, Gilda had Ken wrapped up in a conversation, and Ken told her how he had fallen down the stairs, who he accused of pushing him and the others, and how Ryan had dated basically every single attractive woman in the company. Gilda could feel Ken's hatred for the company, how he felt burned out and the obvious jealousy he had of Ryan. Gilda quietly snickered as Ken compared himself to James Stewart in the movie 'Rear Window', since he was so bored and had been watching everyone from his wheelchair — mostly in the restaurant but also at the pool or from his balcony, facing the pool.

Gilda could be so charming that she ended up sitting at the same table as Ken and three other male VT Tech employees, shooting the breeze. She told them stories about Key West and gave them recommendations as they told her about their vacation and drank countless mimosas. All four men became still when Ryan entered the dining room and walked up to the buffet. Due to his success with the ladies, he was not too popular among men and most of the group thought he'd killed Samantha who had been very needy and obviously wanted him back. Gilda walked up to the buffet and tried to start a conversation with him. "Oh, I'm sorry," she exclaimed as she helped him wipe some crumbs off his shirt from a croissant that had flown from her plate against his chest. "Aren't you one of the members of the tech group with all the accidents happening?"

"Yes." He looked at her with a quizzical expression on his face. "And you are?"

Gilda wasn't prepared for this and now scrambled for an explanation.

"Oh, I'm staying here as well, but I'm a freelance journalist," she said as vaguely as she could. "That's why I'm very interested in the case."

The prospect of someone writing about him immediately sparked Ryan's interest.

"Would you mind answering a few questions?" she asked. "Maybe I can come up with something for this week's edition of Key West Weekly."

"I'd love to," he replied and followed her to an

empty table. Gilda looked around, hoping none of the employees would recognize her and say something, but everyone was busy and minding their own business.

"By the way, I'm Gilda... um, Miller. It's nice to meet you." She stretched her hand out to shake his hand.

He returned the handshake. "Ryan Goslan. Nice to meet you."

A server came up and poured them two new cups of coffee. She recognized Gilda and greeted her. Gilda held her breathe for a moment, but the server didn't find it unusual that Gilda was sitting there with a guest. Gilda exhaled, relieved, and asked Ryan the first, quite explosive question. "So, it seems some of the coworkers have been attacked already and some haven't. Do you think that that makes some a suspect?"

She could tell he didn't like the question since he didn't want to openly accuse any of his coworkers. He was about to answer, when Charles stepped into the dining room, followed by Officers Sanchez and Brinkmann. Those were the last people Gilda wanted to run into while she was talking to Ryan. She said hastily, "I'll be right back," jumped up, walked toward the buffet and around it until she was behind the omelette station and out of sight. The three looked around for a second, then Charles led the two police officers straight toward Ryan who was sitting there watching Gilda leave, his mouth still open mid-sentence. Charles left discreetly.

"Good morning, Mr. Goslan," said Bianca. "We need you to accompany us to the police station to answer some questions regarding the death of Ms. Berg, please."

Ryan's face paled. "Can't I answer those questions right here? Why do I have to go to the police station?"

"This is not a request, Mr. Goslan, it's an order. You need to either come with us voluntarily or we will handcuff you right here, if you'd like to go that route, in front of your coworkers," replied Officer Brinkmann, looking at the other table with Ken and the others. Of course, they were all staring with bated breath.

Ryan had no choice but to accompany Officers Sanchez and Brinkmann. He wasn't having a very good day.

Chapter Twenty-One

The police SUV stopped in front of the police station on Roosevelt Blvd. Officers Sanchez and Brinkmann, as well as Ryan, got out and stepped inside the brand-new pink and white two-story building. Ryan was led to a small interrogation room and offered coffee and water.

Bianca started the interrogation, cutting right to the chase.

"So, Mr. Goslan, we had Ms. Dumas' dive equipment examined by our forensics department, and it looks like someone tampered with her regulator's gauge. You were her dive buddy and closest to her during the entire dive. So, any idea how that got broken? Did you happen to bring a dive knife while scuba diving or anything else that could have broken the gauge? Also, one of the other divers said you were in the stern of the boat with all the dive equipment by yourself for a while. May we ask what you were doing there?"

Ryan was so upset, he almost stood up from his chair as he answered, nearly yelling, veins popping out on the sides of his neck.

"You're not seriously accusing me of trying to kill Lillian, are you? Any possibility that the gauge was already broken before we left? Why would I have rescued her with my octopus then? She's my girlfriend. I love her! And there were three other guys from our company on the boat, all of them lower ranking in the 'top ten' than her! Every single one of them could be a suspect! And about me being in the back with the dive equipment by myself: I was just checking if everything was okay with my gear. Is that not allowed? I hadn't gone diving in a while and was a bit nervous."

"The problem is you also had the strongest motive to kill Ms. Berg. Was she really starting to get on your nerves because she wanted to win you back? Were both women really getting on your nerves with their fight over you? It must've infuriated you that they were both higher ranking than you, usually the number one. Missing out on a hundred thousand dollars when you're used to winning them every year? That's quite a strong motive, Mr. Goslan. And, also, if you checked the dive equipment, why didn't you see that Ms. Dumas' gauge was faulty?"

"That seems like an issue that wouldn't come up until the diver is under water, using the air. I didn't do anything, and I'm not saying another word without my lawyer," he said and slammed his cup of coffee so hard on the table that some of the contents splattered out. "I also have an alibi for the night Samantha died. I was with Lillian."

Bianca and Michael looked at each other over his

head. Unfortunately, he was right, and Lillian had already confirmed the alibi, although, of course, she had been asleep most of the night. They weren't going to be able to detain him, unless they could prove he was guilty.

"We're not going to hold you. We need to return to the hotel. Would you like us to give you a ride?" Bianca asked. Ryan had had it and didn't want to have more to do with the police than he needed to.

"No, thank you. I'll walk."

Everything in Key West was so close that it wasn't more than a ten-minute walk back to the boat shuttle, and maybe he'd run into Lillian if he walked over to Duval Street. She was probably shopping.

The three of them left the building together. Ryan headed down the sidewalk, holding his phone up to his ear as he tried to call Lillian again and again, while Officers Sanchez and Brinkmann drove back to the shuttle to Little Orchid Island.

Kelly, still at her desk in the lobby, was surprised to see them return so quickly, but without Ryan. *Has he been arrested?* she wondered.

The officers nodded at Kelly, who had barely moved from her desk the entire time. She was busy doing paperwork and preparing files and information for her successor. The officers walked up to the front desk and asked for Lillian Dumas' room number. Claire typed her name into her computer, looked at them, and said, "I'm sorry, that guest checked out approximately half an hour ago."

They were baffled. "What?" Bianca asked.

"She departed," repeated Claire. "She also used our airport shuttle."

The police officers ran out to the dock, but once again, the shuttle situation proved to be very inconvenient in case of emergencies. The boat was on the Key West side and wasn't due to be back and depart for another ten minutes. Bianca called their colleagues at the station and ordered, "We are looking for possible murder-suspect Lillian Dumas in the Samantha Berg case. She is supposedly on her way to or at the airport, destination unknown, possibly California. Please send a car over and search the departure terminal. I'll text you a photo as soon as I have one." She quickly went onto Facebook, searched for Lillian Dumas, and found her profile right away. There weren't too many Lillian Dumas, and she didn't have any privacy settings, so anyone could look at the various posts of her posing with Ryan at the pool bar of the Casa Bella, at the beach, on Duval Street or on the dive boat. There were also several photos of Lillian Dumas on VT Tech's website. Officer Sanchez took a screen shot and texted it to her coworkers in their car, heading to the airport.

Leaving head over heels like this put Lillian Dumas back on top of the list of suspects, and Officers Sanchez and Brinkmann were eager to catch her before she left Key West.

"Darn, I feel so helpless," said Bianca as she and Michael stood there, waiting for the shuttle to take them to the mainland and impatiently looking at the time on their phones. The shuttle was going to be here any minute, but it felt like forever, since they were in such a hurry.

Kelly came running up to them.

"Hi, officers, I wanted to tell you about a big fight between Mr. Goslan and Ms. Dumas this morning."

Both officers perked their ears.

"She came running down the stairs, and he followed her. It was hard not to listen, because they were quite loud. She yelled at him, calling him a prick, asking if he had killed Samantha and whether she was next. It was quite the scene. Then she ran out of the hotel toward the shuttle, and he grabbed her arm and tried to hold her back. As the captain walked up to them, he let go of her…"

"Did you see her come back and then check out?"

"No, I must've stepped away for a few minutes to use the bathroom or get a coffee."

Officers Sanchez and Brinkmann looked at each other. Should they have kept Goslan in custody? They needed to question Lillian Dumas even more urgently now. Or had she left because of her fight with Ryan Goslan?

They thanked Kelly and climbed into the shuttle that had finally arrived.

Chapter Twenty-Two

L illian Dumas grabbed her purse and her carry-on, stepped out of the fifteen-passenger hotel shuttle-van and gave the driver a tip. She walked up to the car rental counter inside the small airport's terminal. She didn't want to have to deal with making new flight arrangements and just wanted to get away from her narcissistic, mentally abusive boyfriend and her other hateful coworkers. Lillian really wasn't sure if he had killed Samantha or not. She had slept all night and it would've been easy for him to sneak out of the room, push Samantha off the balcony, and come back. Ryan could be so hateful that Lillian believed he was capable of murder. She wasn't even sure if he had maybe also destroyed her regulator's gauge. Maybe he had chickened out as she was staring at him under water and then helped her with his octopus.

After doing all the paperwork and handing the rental agent her driver's license and credit card, she stepped into the parking garage and walked between the rows of rental cars until she found hers. Her heart did a leap when she saw that she had been upgraded to a nice red Mustang convertible. Lillian had been begging Ryan to leave earlier or stay longer and go for a drive up the Keys; she had heard how beautiful the drive was and had always wanted to see or stay at The Moorings, the gorgeous main location of the TV series 'Bloodline'. Lillian pulled out of the airport and put on a pair of designer sunglasses. She took a left onto South Roosevelt Boulevard, heading toward A1A, the Overseas Highway. The ocean to the right glistened behind swaying palm trees. Lillian heaved a sigh of relief to leave the mess with Ryan and her other coworkers behind at the Casa Bella.

Just about two minutes after Lillian had left, a police car rushed up the airport's entrance, stopped with squealing tires, and two officers jumped out. They ran into the building, showed Lillian's photo to airline employees, then checked the departure board and all six gates. They even looked in the bathrooms and the parking garage, but to no avail. Officers Sanchez and Brinkmann arrived a few minutes later and heard the news. Bianca was angry and snarled at the other police officers. "How could she get away like that?"

Michael saw the car rental counters and had an idea. "Have they been asked? Maybe she's driving and not flying."

Bianca rushed up to the Avis counter and held up her phone with Lillian's photo.

"Hi." She looked at the employee's name tag. "Rita, have you seen this woman in the past half hour?"

"Oh, yes! Very nice lady! She just rented a car for three days with drop-off in Miami half an hour ago." Bianca rolled her eyes. They'd lost precious minutes again. "Can you give me the make and model as well as license plate number of the car?"

"Sure." Rita called up the rental information on her computer, but she was on island time and took a while. Bianca rolled her eyes impatiently. "Sorry, Rita, we're really in a hurry, we need to get this lady."

"Oh, sorry," Rita said and typed a bit faster. "Okay, here it is... Lillian Dumas. She got upgraded to a Mustang convertible."

"Do you have the color?"

"Yes, red. Here's the license plate, XY5 6K9."

"That'll be easy to spot," Bianca said to Michael, then thanked the employee. "Or not. There are probably tons of red mustangs driving around the Keys."

Bianca typed the license plate number into the notes on her smart phone, shared it with Michael and called her colleague, Officer Isabel Baldwin, at the police station in Marathon.

"Hey, Isabel, this is Bianca in Key West, we have an emergency and need your help. One of the main witnesses in the murder case at the Casa Bella who we were just going to take in for questioning has disappeared. She's in a red Mustang convertible, headed your way. Can you help and look out for her?"

"Got it," replied Officer Baldwin. "I'll alert my two officers on patrol, and I'll head to the Seven Mile Bridge myself." She was not a woman of many words, but Bianca knew she was absolutely reliable, and she'd stop the car. "I'm sure Ms. Dumas is closer to Marathon now, but let's drive up that way anyhow. Maybe she stopped somewhere, and we'll see her," she said to Michael. There was only one road, the Overseas Highway, leading in and out of the Keys, so there weren't that many options unless Lillian Dumas was really hiding.

Lillian cruised up the Overseas Highway in the pretty convertible, the sparkling turquoise water on both sides, her hair blowing in the wind. She felt the warm sun tickling her face and her arms and rooted around in her big designer purse for a stylish baseball cap with the VT logo. She drove from Key to Key, crossing bridges, passing beaches, resorts, marinas, oceanfront tiki bars, souvenir shops, residential neighborhoods, and beautiful patches of untouched nature. This seemed like a very special place, and Lillian thought about coming back for a week or so.

She pulled into a little parking lot before the next bridge, got out of the car, and just stood at the railing, watching a pelican dive into the water and fly away with its prey in its pouch. She had no idea that the police in the Keys were frantically looking for her and was finally starting to relax and enjoy her time off for the first time in days, without her hateful and competitive coworkers. Then she stopped again right before the Seven Mile Bridge, in a small parking lot on the Gulf side, and took in the views again.

In this instance, Officer Baldwin drove off the Seven Mile Bridge and missed Lillian's car because it was sandwiched between two bigger trucks. That's how Lillian made it through Marathon and to The Moorings without being seen by anyone, leaving the police flabbergasted.

A few miles down the road, on Bahia Honda Key, Officers Baldwin, Sanchez and Brinkmann rendezvoused, got out of their cars on the shoulder, and shook hands. They had to admit they'd somehow missed Ms. Dumas. Officer Sanchez was fuming. "By now she could be anywhere. I'll call our colleagues in Key Largo and ask them to look out for the red Mustang."

Chapter Twenty-Three

Kelly, in the old beaten up truck Max had kindly lent her, drove down the bumpy, unpaved driveway in between tall bamboo and palm trees, leading to the beautiful resort, The Moorings. It was famous for having been the main location of the TV series 'Bloodline'. The resort had always been very upscale and popular, but since then it became even fancier and a popular fan destination.

Kelly had been making some phone calls and already had a job interview, since the resort was urgently looking to fill the concierge position. She knew the front desk manager and the current concierge from arranging trips to The Moorings. It was quite far from Key West, but it would probably be more affordable to find housing in and around Islamorada.

As the road ended, she parked her car in a small parking lot and walked through the former coconut plantation under rows of palms and past beautiful gardens up to the first lovely cottage with a sign that said *Office*. She walked up the two steps onto a little porch and knocked at the front door.

A female voice called, "Come in!" The young property manager, Kelly's age and a longtime friend of hers, Susan Zalewski, stood up, walked around her desk, and gave Kelly a big bear hug.

"Long time no see," she said cheerfully and looked at Kelly. "You look great! What makes you want to leave the Casa Bella? Is Charles hitting on you?"

That was meant to be a joke, but she had hit the nail on the head. Kelly didn't want to talk about it, which probably would have been unprofessional.

She just gave Susan a blank stare and tried to sound casual. "It's time for a change." Susan knew she was right but didn't insist on going further into detail. Charles' reputation was known in the Keys, and gossip between the hotel employees traveled fast. Susan knew Kelly would eventually pour her heart out. She could tell that she was upset.

"Well, I don't have to tell you about the property, you basically know everything. Our concierge Diane has her last day in ten days, so you could start any time around then, maybe she could train you a little. But I'm sure there's not that much to train. I know you're the best!"

Susan told Kelly a bit about the salary and benefits, which were both about the same as her current job, and they chatted for a few more minutes. Finally, Kelly asked, "Can you give me a day or two to think about it?"

She was now extremely torn between this position and the idea of freelancing and moving in with Gilda and helping her with the kitten. She'd be doing the same thing she'd been doing for the last few years, while freelancing was a different, interesting perspective but also financially a bit risky and nerve-racking. She had some savings, but they would dwindle quickly if she didn't generate enough income. She knew it would take a while to become established and accumulate a regular clientele, and she'd probably need a car if she had to go shopping for clients.

"Of course, I have a few other applicants, but you know you're my first choice," Susan replied. "So, take your time, think about it for a couple of days, and let me know."

They both nodded, and Susan accompanied Kelly out of the building. They stepped onto the beach, chit-chatting about this and that.

"Oh, we finally finished the new dock where weddings and other events can take place. It turned out nice. Are you interested in seeing it? Remember, the old one was destroyed by hurricane Irma?"

In 2017, Hurricane Irma, a category 4 storm, hit the mid Florida Keys with full force, causing a widespread path of destruction, damaging homes and hotels, and taking many lives. It was the most intense hurricane to strike the continental United States since Katrina in 2005.

"Yes, I'd love to see it," Kelly replied and smiled. Fixing all the hurricane damage had taken years, and she knew how happy and relieved the locals were to be rebuilding things. They walked down the perfectly crescent-shaped manmade beach and passed some guests in lounge chairs under beautiful palm trees leaning into the wind. A female guest in a pretty, flowery bikini had just arrived and was applying sunscreen to her arms and legs. The two women's eyes met, and Kelly did a double take. Wasn't that Lillian Dumas from the VT Tech group?

It was, indeed, Lillian, who didn't know whether she wanted the ground to open and swallow her or whether she should pretend everything was fine. She had no choice, though, because Kelly had already stopped to greet her.

"Oh, hi, Ms. Dumas," said Kelly, "I didn't know you're spending the day here."

"I checked out. I had to get away from my boyfriend, or let's rather say ex-boyfriend, for a while. I'd appreciate if you wouldn't tell him that you saw me here," Lillian replied. "I guess you're one of the people who saw the embarrassing argument this morning."

Kelly nodded. "Of course, I won't say anything. It's none of my business anyhow. Enjoy your stay. Isn't it beautiful here?"

"Yes, I'm so glad I came, I've always wanted to. It's like a tropical paradise."

They all smiled. Kelly and Susan said goodbye to Lillian and continued walking down the beach.

Kelly had witnessed Officers Sanchez and Brinkmann speaking with the front desk about Ms. Dumas this morning and finding out that she had checked out early. She pretended to be calm, but as soon as they were far enough away to not be heard by

Lillian Dumas anymore, Kelly looked at Susan and blurted out, "I think the police are looking for that woman!"

Chapter Twenty-Four

Kelly walked back to the truck and called the number of the Key West police station and left a message for Officers Sanchez and Brinkmann about Lillian being at The Moorings. Then she called Gilda and told her the news about running into Lillian Dumas at The Moorings.

"Do you think she killed Samantha Berg?" asked Gilda. Their heads were spinning.

"Not sure. After seeing that scene this morning, I think Mr. Goslan might be abusive. She looked a bit scared when she saw me and asked me not to tell him about our encounter."

Kelly turned the key in the ignition, but the truck just made choking sounds and wouldn't start. She tried again. She sighed and said, "Darn. Sorry, Gilda, I'm going to have to call you back. The truck isn't starting."

"Oh no," said Gilda. "Keep me posted."

Kelly tried starting the truck again. It sputtered and choked but wouldn't start. It would be most inconvenient to get stuck here, almost two hours away from Key West. She finally gave up and called Max who was at work and didn't answer his phone. She didn't know who to call, so she called Gilda again and asked for advice. Gilda looked at her watch.

"Hmmm. It's too late for Ricky to come and pick you up. His concert starts in three hours. Let me think about it. I'll call you back." Just as Gilda and Kelly had ended the call, Officers Sanchez and Brinkmann drove into the parking lot looking for Lillian Dumas after receiving Kelly's message. They stopped next to Kelly who had gotten out of the truck and was about to walk back to the resort.

"Hey, Kelly. Thanks for your message. Do you need help?"

"Maybe. The truck won't start. I think it's the ignition."

"Let me check it out," said Officer Brinkmann as he jumped out of the police SUV. He grabbed the keys from Kelly and got into the driver's seat. The truck choked and sputtered but wouldn't start. "Yeah, I agree, it must be the ignition. The bad news is you'll probably need to have it towed."

Kelly felt awful that this had happened while she had borrowed the truck. But, most importantly, she was stuck here.

"We can give you a ride back to Key West," said Officer Sanchez. "But we must go and get Ms. Dumas first. This isn't going to be pleasant."

"We'd appreciate if you could wait here. The less audience the better."

The two officers turned around and walked toward the resort. Kelly leaned against the truck and called Gilda to let her know she had a ride.

"Do you have to leave the truck there?"

"Yeah, Officer Brinkmann agrees that it's the ignition and has to be towed."

"My brother lives up there in Islamorada and owns a car repair place. He can do it for a good price," said Gilda. This was a sneak peek of how many contacts Gilda had all over the Keys and how helpful she was. "Hide the key on one of the tires or under the visor. That way you won't have to be there tomorrow when my brother tows it."

Kelly was extremely thankful for that idea. "I would have never thought of that. Thanks, Gilda."

Soon, Officers Brinkmann and Sanchez returned with a very unhappy Lillian Dumas.

"You guys are ruining my vacation! This hotel is expensive! And, under no circumstances do I want to see Ryan again or him to know where I am!"

"I'm sorry, but according to the judge's order, which I showed you, you are an indispensable witness and not allowed to leave town. We assure you that we won't mention you to Mr. Goslan." Lillian was mad, but she knew she couldn't refuse.

Officers Brinkmann and Sanchez got in the front of the SUV, Kelly and Lillian in the back. Lillian looked at Kelly full of hate in her eyes. "Are you the one who told them I'm here?"

"Now, Ms. Dumas, please calm down," Officer Sanchez interrupted. "Ms. Palmer has nothing to do with this. She's just here by coincidence."

Lillian Dumas huffed, threw one last angry glance at Kelly, then she looked out of the window. Kelly remained silent. What could have been a fun drive back to Key West for her ended up not being pleasant, but she was thankful to get back home.

As they got closer to Key West, Bianca's phone rang. She answered.

"Bernard here."

"Hey, Thomas, hang on a sec. Let me take you off speakerphone. We're not alone in the car." She looked in the rearview mirror and saw Lillian and Kelly, both silently looking out of the windows, but they were probably listening.

"Go ahead, Thomas," she said.

"The tox screen showed that Samantha Berg had no antidepressants in her blood. So, she was either not taking her antidepressants or they were switched out for placebos." He paused and then shared the even bigger news. "But, more importantly, the HCG level in her blood shows that she was pregnant."

"Wow," replied Bianca. She looked at Michael from the side and made a face.

He, of course, was dying to hear the news, but she couldn't speak with the two women in the vehicle.

"Thomas, can I call you back in about twenty minutes? We have Lillian Dumas with us in the car and Kelly from the Casa Bella. Long story."

"Sure. Call me back."

Bianca looked at Michael, who was driving. "Please speed up a little." But then she corrected herself because they were driving through Key Deer habitat.

"Actually don't speed up, watch out for Key Deer."

From the expression on her face, Michael could tell that she had just gotten very important news. He stepped on the gas pedal, and as they came to a red light, he turned the flashing lights on and drove through, slowing down just a little to make sure the crossing traffic stopped for them. Also, he made sure to keep an eye out for Key deer which could be found in this area and were endangered.

The sun was setting when the officers dropped Kelly off at her apartment. She rushed inside, took a shower, packed a backpack full of things, and was on her way to Gilda's house. She had called Gilda's brother from the road. Max's truck was already being towed to a garage and was going to be ready for pickup tomorrow afternoon. Max was informed that he wouldn't have his truck until tomorrow, but he didn't need it anyhow when he was working. He offered to help Kelly pick it up, but it wasn't going to be ready until his shift started, so she'd have to find a different solution.

The officers continued to the police station, assisted Lillian Dumas into a small interrogation room and asked her to wait for a few minutes.

They walked over to their office, where Bianca told Michael what Bernard had informed her about. If this was murder, the fact that Samantha Berg had been pregnant made the case even more heinous. And if Ryan was the father, that would give him yet another motive. Bianca pressed Bernard's number, which she had on speed dial.

"Thomas, it's me again. So, can we find out who the father was?"

"Yes, we can do DNA-testing. We need a DNA sample from the possible father. Are we talking about Ryan Goslan?"

"Yes. We'll take care of that," replied Bianca "Thanks, Thomas."

She looked at Michael. "I'll stay with Ms. Dumas, and you go to Casa Bella and take Ryan Goslan back in. "If he refuses, arrest him. He's back to being suspect number one."

Chapter Twenty-Five

Ricky and his band were already playing as Kelly jumped out of the Old Key West Trolley she had taken to be faster and walked up to the restaurant at the end of Duval Street. She was wearing a fun tropical sundress that accentuated her green eyes and was happy about that. It made her feel comfortable and attractive.

The band was set up on a stage in a corner of the open-air dining area, and the whole garden and walkway leading up to the venue were full of people. The band consisted of Ricky playing tenor saxophone, a trumpet player, a drummer, a bass player, and a piano player. Ricky was currently trading solos with the trumpet player to a very uplifting and fast Latin tune. They kept taking turns as if talking to each other or arguing. People cheered and danced. Kelly could feel Ricky's charisma and felt compelled to start dancing too. He looked hot playing the saxophone in his Hawaiian shirt and faded jeans. Kelly recognized that the trumpet player was Alex, the friend who had been at Gilda's house the other night. Finally, the solo was over, and the percussionist took over, this time on a pair of congas. He improvised in a perfect rhythm, hitting the congas faster and faster until it didn't even seem humanly possible that he could be playing that fast. He rose to a crescendo, and then he suddenly stopped. The crowd hooted and hollered. The percussionist started up again slowly, and Ricky and the trumpet player took over for a grand finale.

Suddenly, Gilda stepped up to Kelly and pulled her closer to the stage where the musicians were taking a bow and thanking the audience. Ricky smiled at Kelly and his mom. Kelly felt her heart flutter and smiled back.

Ricky, who was obviously the bandleader, introduced the musicians and announced: "Thank you, ladies and gentlemen. We're going to take a short break of fifteen minutes and will be back for our second set."

"Wow, they're really good!" Kelly said to Gilda, excited. "I wish I hadn't missed almost the entire first set, but I was lucky to get a ride back!" She had already filled Gilda in about Lillian Dumas being taken back to Key West by Officers Sanchez and Brinkmann.

"I'm glad you made it at all. Did Jose call you back about the truck?"

"Yes, I already spoke with his guy in the garage too. It'll be done by tomorrow afternoon, but I need to figure out how to pick it up."

Gilda thought for a second and already had an idea.

"Ricky is heading back to Orlando tomorrow afternoon. He could drop you off and then you drive the truck back. We'll ask him later."

Kelly hated to impose, but it did seem like a good solution.

Gilda and Kelly made their way to the bar to get a drink and say hi to Ricky, who was getting himself a beer.

"Great solo, Ricky! Remember Kelly?"

"How could I not remember Kelly!" He looked at her with a big smile and kissed her on the cheek, which made Kelly's knees weak. Then he kissed his mother as well who took him in her arms and gave him a big bear hug. Kelly could tell that Gilda was very proud of him, a nice thing to see.

"Well, I have to get back on stage," said Ricky. "Thanks for coming, Mom, Kelly." Kelly liked his good manners. She and Gilda made their way back toward the stage and waited for the musicians to return. The crowd was already whistling and cheering impatiently. The musicians stepped back onto the stage and, without wasting time, they started playing another fun Latin piece that reminded Kelly of Santana. She looked around the happy crowd, which consisted of tourists as well as locals, and realized how this event had distracted her from her heartache over Charles and the things going on at the hotel. *How could I have been missing all this?* she thought. There was probably something like this going on every day in Key West. Kelly had not been living life to its fullest and knew she had to change that.

She looked at Gilda, who was happily moving to the rhythm, and started dancing herself. The concert was over much too soon, and Kelly found herself walking home with Gilda and Ricky, his saxophone case in his hand. She was excited about the jazz they'd been playing, something her parents used to listen to a lot, and bombarded him with questions. It just seemed amazing that from a very young age, he'd already known that he wanted to be a musician and had stuck with it while other people switched from major to major and still didn't know what they wanted to do.

"We could tell that he was talented from a young age and always encouraged him to follow his heart," said Gilda, looking proudly at Ricky. "He made All-State every single year, which means he was one of the best saxophone players in Florida in his age."

Ricky was quite down to earth and became embarrassed when his mother started bragging.

"Ma, that's enough. I just love it and work hard," he said modestly.

Kelly grinned. She got that Gilda was proud of Ricky and replied, "Your mom has all the right to brag. You sounded amazing."

He smiled at her and looked down.

Kelly noticed his long, thick eyelashes and wanted to melt away.

Within ten minutes they arrived at the house and immediately checked on Zoë the kitten. She was sitting at the door of the crate, meowing pitifully, probably hungry.

"Wow, it looks like she's grown in the last twenty-four hours," said Kelly, amazed.

"She has a really good appetite," replied Gilda. "Why don't you get her out and try to stimulate her butt so she can pee? I'll go and make her milk."

Not a task Kelly was looking forward to, but she knew she had to learn it, so she got the tiny little kitten out of her crate. The poor thing was meowing non-stop and started suckling at her finger, so Kelly held her for a little bit first to give the motherless kitten some love and body warmth. She seemed to like it and calmed down. Then Kelly held her with one hand above the pad on the bathroom counter and massaged her bottom with the other hand. In this instance, Ricky stepped into the bathroom. He had been starving and needed to eat something first, but he had already fallen in love with the kitten and had to check on her. Kelly noticed a yellow spot on the pad and exclaimed, "Yay, she peed!" Then she was a bit embarrassed to shout that out with this strange guy in the bathroom. Ricky, however, didn't make the situation awkward at all and joined in her happiness.

"Mom has been having a hard time with that, that's great news!"

Gilda came in and celebrated that the kitten had peed as well. Then she handed Ricky the bottle and said, "I need to answer some urgent emails regarding the orchid society meeting tomorrow. "Can you show Kelly how to do this, Ricky?"

Ricky wanted to do nothing rather than that. "I'm the cat whisperer," he said, grinning proudly, and Kelly watched the kitten knead his chest with her two front paws as if preparing a nest. Once again, her heart was melting, not only because of the kitten, but also because of this sensitive young man who was also extremely handsome with his head of thick dark curly hair, long thick eyelashes, full lips, and chiseled chin. She couldn't help but wonder how many girls had a crush on him.

Ricky checked the warmth of the milk in the bottle his mother had given him just like for a baby. He dripped a couple of drops on his wrist. It was fine. Then he held the kitten sideways on the bathroom counter and held the bottle so that it was facing down toward the kitten's mouth. The kitten started sucking the nipple eagerly, but it kept ending up biting it. Ricky kept pulling it away until the kitten had properly latched on to the bottle and was drinking properly. "It seems cruel to keep taking it away, but it's going to ruin the nipple by biting holes into it," he explained.

"Now you try." He got up, handed Kelly the kitten and the bottle and gave her instructions as she sat down and imitated what he had just showed her. It wasn't easy, but finally the kitten had drunk almost an ounce of milk and was full. It now wanted to play and explore and crawled across the bathroom floor.

"The hardest part is to get her back to sleep in the middle of the night. Cats are quite nocturnal," said Ricky. "I can take turns with you tonight if you want," he proposed and looked at the time on his phone. "It's ten now. You do the next feeding at one, and I'll do the four a.m. one, then you do seven again."

Ricky looked at Kelly and continued. "It sounds like a lot, but it's only for about two weeks, then we can do one feeding around midnight and the next one at seven. My mom has done it before. It's worth it because these kittens become affectionate cats when they're older."

They were just putting Zoë back into the crate when Gilda popped back in.

"Ricky, do you think you can give Kelly a ride to Jose's garage in Islamorada tomorrow afternoon? She needs to pick up a truck there and that would work out well with your drive back up to Orlando."

Ricky looked at Kelly. He kind of liked the idea of being in a car with her for two hours tomorrow. It almost seemed like a date.

"Sure."

"Thanks," said Kelly. She felt the same way. It didn't seem like a bad thing being stuck with him in a car for two hours…

Gilda saw the sparks flying and popped her head back out. "Good night, guys," she said as she walked back down the hallway toward her bedroom.

Chapter Twenty-Six

Meanwhile at the Casa Bella, there was a loud scream from a male voice on the second floor. Kevin, the assistant front desk manager on duty, ran up the stairs and found Conor Mitchum, number five of the ten VT Tech group VIPs, standing unharmed, yet very shaken up at the top of the staircase. He was as pale as a sheet and pointed at the staircase leading up to the third floor. Even though he didn't really believe in ghosts, he insisted that one had just rushed past him, pushed him, and run up to the third floor.

"It seemed like just a shadow, not a real person. But it was definitely female, in a long white robe and with long blonde hair."

Even though he knew the story sounded crazy, he insisted on calling the police, since he thought he was supposed to be pushed down the stairs. "Just like my colleague Ken," he said, still panting. "This is seriously creepy. I think we need police protection." Unbeknownst to him, they already had police protection, but of course that undercover officer, couldn't be everywhere at the same time. He had been sitting at the pool bar, hanging out with Ken. Minutes later, as he noticed the commotion in the main building, Officer Ralph Stone looked up with a guilty conscience. Instead of making his rounds on the property and paying attention to what was going on, he had been shooting the breeze with one of the guests. He ran into the lobby to check what was going on, slowly followed by Ken in his wheelchair.

"I'm Officer Stone," he introduced himself to Conor Mitchum while getting his ID out of his wallet and holding it up. "I've been on the premises since yesterday, keeping an eye on things, while trying not to attract too much attention to myself. Can you please tell me what happened and if you're okay?"

"Oh, hi, Officer," said Conor, a bit embarrassed to have made such a scene. "Sorry to yell like that, but I was really scared there for a second. I almost fell down the stairs, just like Ken. I can't afford to sit in a wheelchair for weeks – or break my neck, if I dare say."

Officer Stone nodded. "I totally understand. Anyone would be in shock."

"So, I was coming down from the third floor, and as I was about to step onto the stairs leading down to the first floor, I saw a white shadow out of the corner of my eye, and I was pushed – really hard. So hard that I'd almost say it was a guy if I hadn't seen her face and long hair."

Officers Sanchez and Brinkmann, who had been informed immediately and had been lucky to catch the boat shuttle right away, walked up at the same time as

Ken rolled up on his wheelchair. They heard what Conor said, and everyone looked puzzled.

"Hi, ...Mr.?" said Bianca.

"Mitchum. Conor Mitchum."

"Are you hurt?"

He shook his head.

Can you fill us in, Stone?"

"It almost seems to me that we might be dealing with a man, dressed up as a female ghost, who's pushing people in the group. At least that's what just happened."

"What are we waiting for then? Follow me!" barked Bianca and rushed up the stairs, followed by Officers Brinkmann and Stone, to the third floor and searched the hallway. At the end of the hallway, she came up to an old wooden door that looked different than the room doors. She opened the door and stood in front of another set of old creaky stairs leading onto a small rooftop terrace.

Of course, it was too late, and nobody was there anymore, but she found a small piece of white gauze that had obviously been torn off another piece of fabric, as the "ghost" probably escaped down a fire ladder leading down the side of the building. Bianca put on a pair of plastic gloves and got a little bag out of her back pocket. She carefully slid the piece of evidence into the bag and handed it to Michael who had just stepped onto the terrace with Officer Stone.

"Please get this to forensics ASAP and have it examined for fingerprints."

She continued, "So, there obviously really is a

ghost. But it's not the famous author's former mistress. It's someone dressing up as her."

The two men were flabbergasted but nodded.

The police returned the next morning and did a more accurate search of the property and the rooftop terrace again. They took fingerprints from the doorhandle leading to the rooftop terrace, the fire escape, and the entire area around the fire escape on the ground which was very close to the side employee entrance leading into the kitchen.

Max was in the kitchen this morning. He had just received a delivery of fresh grouper and watched the police officers at work. Bianca asked him, "You're Max Freeman, the head chef, right?"

He nodded, not very happy to be dealing with the police. This was outside of his working hours, and he wanted to get back home as quickly as possible. And he didn't want anyone to know that he used to work at VT Tech and hated them.

"Does anyone ever use this fire ladder or the rooftop terrace? It's quite close to your kitchen entrance. Wouldn't that be a nice place for a break?"

Max didn't feel like talking to her and just said, "not really," but in that instance Charles, who had heard the question, walked up, and jumped in.

"The fire ladder is not so popular. It's quite hard to

climb up, you need a lot of arm strength. "But the rooftop terrace is a not-so-secret romantic spot for guests and employees. It's officially off-limits though since it's quite dangerous up there. The floor and the railings are old and brittle and in need of renovation. I don't know if you noticed the signs up there. They say to "keep out."

"Thank you, Charles," said Bianca. She watched Max walk back into the kitchen, wondering why he had been so unpleasant.

"Not a man of many words, especially early in the morning," explained Charles shrugging as they walked around the building and back inside toward the lobby.

An unusually long line of people was standing at the front desk. The front desk employees were obviously overwhelmed and having a hard time taking care of everyone fast enough, so people were grumbling and starting to complain.

Charles stepped up to them and asked, "Can I help you, ladies and gentlemen? Maybe I can be of assistance?"

They all started talking at the same time.

"We just wanna get out of here!" "So much going on here!" "This place is haunted!" "Another crime last night!"

"There is no need to be nervous, ladies and gentlemen!" said Charles, pretending to be cool and relaxed, even though this was a catastrophe for the hotel's reputation.

"This next to me is our local Chief Inspector, Officer Bianca Sanchez. She will assure you that you are in no danger whatsoever and that everything is being taken care of."

Bianca stepped up next to him. "Everything is under control, ladies and gentlemen. You have nothing to worry about and no reason to be checking out."

But the guests had made up their minds and couldn't be persuaded to stay and remained in the line.

Charles and Bianca kept walking toward his office. Charles rang his hands. "This is a catastrophe," he said. "I'm sure I'm going to hear from the owners again. Please do whatever you can to solve this case, Officer Bianca. My reputation as a manager is at stake."

Bianca nodded and said, "We'll take care of it," trying to pacify him. But she didn't feel so certain. Unless the piece of fabric showed some fingerprints that matched someone, they still had no clue. And it wasn't Ryan Goslan or Lillian Dumas. Lillian had been driven back to The Moorings last night after they hadn't been able to hold her without any proof to arrest her. And Ryan had also been at the police station to give the police a DNA sample last night during the time of the incident. He was still a main suspect but there was no proof to arrest him for murder.

Chapter Twenty-Seven

Kelly helped the overwhelmed front-desk with the unusual amount of check outs. It wasn't fun dealing with the unhappy guests, but she understood where they were coming from. There seemed to be too many unpleasant things going on at the hotel for someone who was paying a lot of money and just wanted to kick back and relax. She walked back to her desk on the other side of the lobby. To her surprise, she found a giant bouquet of flowers with a card that someone had left. She sat down and looked around as she opened the card.

Kelly, everyone deserves a second chance. Please stay! *Love, Charles.*

Kelly stared at the card, disgusted. Why couldn't he understand that she needed to get away from him and let her go? Wednesday was her last day, and she couldn't wait to not have to see him every day anymore. Her crush had turned into dislike, but she tried to stay professional in case she might want to freelance for this hotel in the future. She grabbed the vase with the bouquet, walked over to the front desk, and set it down.

"I thought this might cheer you guys up a little after dealing with all those unhappy guests," she said to Claire.

Claire had watched Charles put the bouquet on Kelly's desk and understood. She smiled and discreetly said, "Thank you!"

Little did Kelly know that at this exact moment Charles was being fired. The situation at the hotel wasn't really his fault, but the owners were very unhappy and needed someone to blame. New management would make the hotel look better once this nightmare with the VT Tech group was over...

Gilda, whose hours were a bit more flexible, stepped into the lobby. Kelly had already texted her about what had happened last night. Gilda sat in front of her, eager to exchange thoughts and discuss the case again. "It is so confusing," said Gilda. "Do you think we're all wrong that we've been accusing Ryan Goslan or Lillian Dumas, and maybe it was... Max? He has long blonde hair, a pretty face, could easily go for a woman in the dark, and hates the VT Tech people? He could have easily dressed up as a ghost and has the arm strength to give someone a hard push and climb up and down the fire ladder."

Kelly nodded. As much as she liked Max, she had also considered him as the possible perpetrator.

"But do you think Max is capable of murder? I can see him being mad and the pushing, but *murder*?"

"Well, it could have been an accident. They could

have had an argument, wrestled and he pushed her over the railing by mistake," said Gilda. "Do you think you should tell Officer Bianca that he used to work for VT Tech?"

Kelly was really torn. Should she be a snitch and turn her friend in? But if she didn't tell, she'd make herself guilty as well by withholding important information. "He's my friend, but I guess I'll have to. I'd be hindering the investigation if I didn't…"

But Kelly didn't have to tell her. Bianca, sitting in the conference room with her colleague Michael, couldn't stop thinking about Max's strange behavior and had already googled him on her phone.

"Bingo!" she said.

There were no secrets on the internet. Not only were there photos of Max Freeman during his time as an employee of VT Tech, but Bianca also found out that three years ago he had been the number-one employee and won the hundred-thousand-dollar award and even that Samantha Berg might have been his girlfriend at some point. It wasn't mentioned anywhere, but she was in a lot of pictures with Max, posing for the camera with him, arm in arm. Just a few months later, Max had suffered a nervous breakdown, obviously from burnout, quit his job, and disappeared from all VT Tech posts and photos.

"How come he became a chef here and rose up the chef career ladder so quickly?" Bianca was thinking out loud, but Michael answered. "Well, the two companies are somehow connected. It seems the hotel owners' son runs VT Tech, so who knows. He might be friends with Max and have helped him."

"Let's take Max in for questioning and fingerprints," said Bianca. They already had the results from their forensics department regarding last night's incident, but there was no match so far.

They both got up and walked over to the kitchen. Max was cutting the grouper delivery into filets in a small separate room leading to the cooling chamber. This wasn't really his job as the chef, but he was a perfectionist and knew exactly how he wanted the pieces cut. Max paled as he saw the two officers entering the room. He looked around, but there was nowhere to escape besides through the main kitchen, which was full of his colleagues working the breakfast shift. And they'd get him somewhere on the island eventually. He knew he was innocent, but he could see that he looked suspicious, and his first impulse was to run away from the police.

"Mr. Freeman, we have to ask you to accompany us to the police station for some questioning and your fingerprints in the Samantha Berg case."

"On what grounds? Am I a suspect now? What gives you that idea?"

"You know the hotel and that rooftop terrace, and you obviously knew Ms. Berg very well. We'd just like to ask you a few questions. The less fuss you make, the less attention you'll draw to yourself. It'll just look like we're coincidently leaving the hotel together."

"Can I finish cutting the grouper? Otherwise, it'll spoil." He pointed at the fish that he was almost done with.

"Sure. Can you be done in five minutes? The next ferry leaves pretty soon."

Max nodded.

Just as Kelly had decided to talk to Officers Sanchez and Brinkman, she saw them walking in front of the hotel toward the boat dock with Max. It looked like they had walked outside around the building coming from the kitchen, and it wasn't clear if Max was walking with the police, but Kelly assumed so. She felt terrible for Max and sighed.

"Gilda, look, it looks like they already had the idea about Max on their own. I really hope he didn't kill Samantha Berg."

Chapter Twenty-Eight

Turns out the fingerprints were not Max's, and he had an alibi for the time during the "ghost incident", which had happened in the evening. He had been working, and several of his colleagues in the kitchen vouched for him. So, he had to be released, even though there was always a slight chance he had snuck away for five minutes... Officers Bianca and Michael were running out of suspects, and Ryan Goslan was number one again. But if it was Ryan Goslan, there had to be several perpetrators because he also had an alibi. He had been at the police station while his colleague Conor Mitchum was attacked. Bianca's and Michael's heads were spinning, and they kept running around in circles. Their chief's boss, the sheriff of Monroe County, was really upset because his four-year term was about to end. He was hoping to get re-elected, and this case was making him look bad in the polls. His opponent was making sure to make a big deal out of the situation and the press was too. Some of his main supporters were the owners of the Casa Bella where lots of his fundraisers and rallies took place. Bianca and Michael kept getting pressure not only from him and the owners of the Casa Bella, who were losing lots of their guests. The hotel's occupancy had never been worse during this time of year.

"We really have no proof to keep Goslan here," said Bianca sighing as she ended a phone call. "That was Bernard. He just got the results of DNA test with Goslan's DNA and told me that Goslan is not the father."

"Maybe we should look for the father," proposed Officer Brinkmann. Bianca nodded. They searched Samantha Berg's room, phone, and laptop again and found some information about a new boyfriend and possible father. But he was in California and was shocked about Samantha's death.

"If only we could find the gown belonging to the piece of gauze," said Bianca.

Michael nodded. They needed something to get the case rolling. "What if we get a search warrant for Goslan's room?" asked Michael. Bianca looked up from her laptop. They were grasping for straws at this point, but it was an idea. She nodded. "Call the judge's office and have them issue a warrant. We need to follow every lead we can get." But searching Ryan Goslan's room didn't lead anywhere. He seemed innocent. He had succumbed to his girlfriend Lillian's disappearance, was bored, and had started day-drinking with his buddy Ken Miller. They were both becoming quite a nuisance for the hotel. They'd either sit in the lobby or by the pool, or in the breakfast room all day with drinks by their sides, making rude comments about other guests or staff. Sometimes Officer Stone would join them since there wasn't much going on at the hotel anymore. Lots of people had checked out because of the incidents, and it was Sunday. The weekend was almost over. The VT Tech employees, now eight without Samantha Berg and Lillian Dumas, were some of the only remaining guests in the hotel.

Kelly's work was slow too, and since she had a lot of overtime, she called Ricky and asked whether he could leave early to drive to Islamorada.

"I'd love that," he replied in an upbeat manner. "I'm ready to go, I was just waiting for you. Do you have to go home first, or shall I pick you up at the shuttle?"

"I do have to go home. I got some cash to pay the repair guy and forgot to bring it with me. Would it be okay for you to meet me there? It's one twenty-three Whitehead. I'm in the guesthouse in the back. Second floor. In half an hour?"

"Sure," he replied. "Looking forward to seeing you."

She suddenly became nervous. They'd be in his car next to each other for almost two hours. Would they have anything to talk about? Would the situation be awkward? However, there wasn't time to fret. She packed her things, let the colleagues at the front desk know she was leaving for the day, and walked out to the shuttle. The shuttle was a bit delayed, so when Kelly got home, Ricky was already waiting in front of her apartment. It was a very awkward situation because Max was sitting out on his little terrace, having coffee. He was ignoring Ricky and not being very friendly. He wasn't too thrilled about this handsome Latin lover asking for Kelly. Kelly realized that Max wasn't too hospitable and introduced them.

"Max, this is Ricky. He's Gilda's son, and he's dropping me off in Islamorada to get your truck since he's driving back to Orlando. It works out perfectly. Any other person would have had to go back and forth."

Max finally relaxed a little. Maybe Ricky wasn't competition, and he was just helping. Max turned into his good old friendly self. He jumped up and shook Ricky's hand.

"Nice to meet you, Ricky. Would you guys like a coffee to go? I'm just getting ready for work and brewed some fresh coffee to get me through the evening..."

He looked a bit suspicious when Ricky walked up to Kelly and kissed her on the cheek, but Kelly replied happily, "I'd love one. Can you wait here for a sec, Ricky? I'll just use the bathroom and get my cash."

Max understood. "Kelly, you don't have to pay for the repair," he said. "It's my beat-up old truck that needs a new part. It's not your fault."

But Kelly insisted. "Well, it happened on my

watch, so I feel responsible," she said.

"Well, we'll figure it out," Max said, then stepped inside his apartment to get three coffees to go.

Ricky and Kelly thanked Max, walked up the driveway and climbed into the shiny older model but nicely kept BMW, which Kelly commented on. "Wow, nice set of wheels!"

Ricky nodded a bit embarrassed. "My mom and grandparents spoil us. Both my sister and I got nice cars when we graduated from high school because they wanted us to be safe driving to and from college." Kelly found that sweet. Gilda was the type of woman who gave all her money to her kids and barely had anything herself. Ricky read Kelly's mind. "My father had a pretty good life insurance when he died and Mom's pretty street smart, so she's not that bad off. Besides her job at all the hotels, she sells a lot of valuable orchids and other plants too. And she has her income from working at the Garden Club."

He fished around the backseat and handed Kelly a bag of fresh pastries with a smile. "These will go perfectly with the coffee. They're from Cole's Peace, my favorite bakery in Key West." Kelly was impressed. How thoughtful of him!

Chapter Twenty-Nine

The BMW left Key West behind and turned onto the Overseas Highway, US1, one of the most beautiful scenic drives in America, also called "the highway that goes to sea." They drove through the lower Keys, turquoise water sprinkled with little islands on both sides of the bridges. The cloudless sky seemed endless, with pelicans, ospreys, and frigate birds darting back and forth. It was one of those days when you just wanted to stop your car on the side of the road, take it all in, and forget about all your troubles.

That's how Kelly felt, and there was not a moment of awkward silence as she had feared. She and Ricky hit it off and had so much to talk about that he almost forgot to stop in Islamorada to drop her off. The almost two-hour drive had passed way too fast, and they could've talked all the way to Orlando.

They pulled into the driveway of an auto body shop at the entrance of a little strip mall. Kelly was thrilled to see that Ricky didn't just drive away and got out of the car with her instead. He wanted to know that she'd have a working car to get back to Key West before he left, and, unbeknownst to Kelly, the repair shop owner was his favorite uncle.

A short older Cuban man with a big gray beard and weathered skin stepped out of the office part of the old concrete building with the words *auto shop* painted on it. He started smiling as he recognized Ricky.

"Hola pequeño!" he ¬said—even though Ricky was a head taller than him—as he walked up to him and gave him a big bear hug. In his memories, Ricky was still a five-year-old munchkin.

"Hola, tio Jose!" He turned around and put his hand on Kelly's shoulder. "This is Kelly. Mama told you about her."

Uncle Jose shook Kelly's hand and smiled. "Nice to meet you. Any friend of Gilda's is my friend too."

"Nice to meet you too. Thank you so much for squeezing the truck in. It's my friend's, so I feel awful it broke down while I had it."

"It happens. It's an old car, so you shouldn't blame yourself. The ignition is brand new now and will probably outlive the rest of the truck," he replied, grinning, and led them over to Max's beat-up truck.

After starting the truck and chit-chatting for a while, Kelly went inside and paid the ridiculously low price for the repair. Then she thanked Ricky profusely for the ride and they said their goodbyes, Ricky sneaking in a little kiss on her cheek again.

Kelly couldn't help it and had to ask, "When are you coming back to visit your mom?"

He looked at her intensely, and her legs weakened

a little. "Probably this weekend. We have another gig in the same bar as the other night. I hope to see you too?"

She nodded, and off he went. He didn't seem to know that they were roommates now when he stayed at his mom's place in Key West. Kelly stood there, holding her hand on her cheek where he had kissed her and just watched the car drive up the Overseas Highway until it was out of sight. Uncle Jose watched her from his office, shaking his head. *Another girl's heart about to be broken,* he thought to himself as he watched Kelly climb into the old pickup and head south.

Kelly saw a break in the oncoming cars on the other side of the road and made a spontaneous decision. She took a left, almost with screeching tires, into The Moorings just as she was about to pass the beautiful resort.

I hope this isn't bad luck, she thought as she stopped in the exact same parking spot she had parked in when the truck broke down. She quickly forgot about the negative thoughts though, jumped out of the truck, and walked down the overgrown tropical path beneath coconut palms over to the office building. She knocked at the door, waited for Susan to shout, "Come in," and then stepped into the cool air-conditioned office. Susan hadn't been expecting Kelly but wasn't very busy and was always happy to see her old friend. She jumped up, walked around the desk, and hugged her.

"Does this surprise visit mean you have good news for me?" she asked, hinting about the concierge position.

Kelly didn't quite know how to say it, but she had to be honest, and the earlier Susan knew, the better.

"I'm so sorry, Susan, but I've decided to stay in Key West and freelance. It's a financial risk, but I just need to do something different for a while."

"Oh, no, that's too bad, but I understand," Susan replied. "You know there's always a position of some type here for you if your plans don't work out and you change your mind. If not as a concierge, you could assist me. We always need good people."

Kelly smiled and gave her a hug. "Thanks, Sue, I really appreciate it."

And just like that, Kelly had made up her mind to become a freelance concierge. She was nervous, yet excited.

"Can you stay for coffee?" asked Susan. "Let's have it outside on the little patio. It's nice and breezy out." Kelly looked at her watch. "Sure, I could use a little afternoon pick-me-up before I head back," she replied.

"Why don't you wait on the patio, and I'll go and make us some lattes."

Kelly stepped out onto the little trail leading to a hidden patio right in front of the beach, only used by employees. As she sat down and checked her messages, she suddenly heard a familiar voice.

"Yeah, she's gone." Kelly listened up. It was obviously Lillian Dumas speaking about Samantha Berg. "I'm number three now. No, Conor's fine."

The person on the other end of the line was obviously talking, and Lillian just said "okay" and "aha" a few times and ended the call.

Susan stepped up with the coffee and some cookies and started a conversation, and Kelly was distracted.

Half an hour later, Kelly needed to get going before rush hour on the busy Overseas Highway started. "Thanks for the coffee," she said. "And, again, sorry about the job. It would have been fun to work with you, but I just feel like my place is in Key West right now."

Susan nodded. She knew it would've been a step back for Kelly to work in the same position at a smaller, less busy resort. "Stay in touch and drive careful."

Kelly suddenly remembered Lillian Dumas and what she had heard. Out of curiosity, she walked down toward the beach to see if she was still somewhere around, but she was gone now. Kelly slowly walked back to the truck, wondering whether she should tell Officers Sanchez and Brinkmann about what she'd heard, got into the truck, and slowly drove toward the main road. There was a break in traffic and, without having to slow down, she pulled out and took a left onto the Overseas Highway. A few hundred yards down the road, traffic was stopped ahead of her, so she had to slow down a little–and suddenly realized that her brakes weren't working. She couldn't stop the truck!

Chapter Thirty

L uckily, the street had a bit of an incline, and Kelly was able to steer the car onto the shoulder where she didn't hit anybody and only rolled into the sand and then gently bumped into a palm tree. The damage was minimal, but Kelly sat there for a few minutes, just breathing, in shock. Two coconuts thumped on the roof and the truck's hood and caused quite the dents, but that and some dents and scratches on the bumper and the palm tree were the entire extent of the damage. Kelly burst into tears, imagining what could have happened. She could be terribly injured and could've caused a bad accident–or driven off a bridge. The car had just been in the garage. How could this happen? Soon, some helpers came running up.

"Miss, are you okay? I'm a nurse. Is there anything I can do? Do you have any medical conditions?" The first helper addressed her while she was still in shock and barely able to answer.

"I think I'm okay. I wasn't going fast at all. The brakes didn't work, and I realized it soon enough."

A police car with flashing lights on the roof

stopped behind the truck, and Officers Isabel Baldwin and her colleague Steve Pratt got out. The onlookers formed a path for them, and they stepped up to the truck. "I'm Officer Baldwin, Marathon PD, and this is my colleague, Steve Pratt. Are you okay, Miss?"

"Yes, I'm fine. The brakes didn't work."

Officer Pratt stepped up. "Can you please get out so I can check the brakes?"

"And why don't you give me your driver's license and registration in the meantime?" asked Officer Baldwin.

Kelly got out of the truck, handed Officer Baldwin the paperwork, and Officer Pratt climbed in to pump the breaks which didn't work. Then he slid under the truck and checked the brake line. He could quickly tell that it had been cut. "Someone cut the brake line," he said, "we should have forensics come and examine this."

Kelly was horrified. "Who would do that? I just stopped briefly at The Moorings, and before I stopped, they were still working. I had just picked the truck up from a garage."

"Is there anyone who could want to harm you?" asked Officer Baldwin.

Kelly couldn't think of anyone spontaneously. "No." But then she thought of the incidents at the hotel and Lillian Dumas, who was staying at The Moorings. But how did Lillian Dumas know that she'd been there? Had she seen her? Kelly mentioned it anyhow.

"This sounds really crazy, but have you heard about all the incidents that have been happening at the

Casa Bella, and about the woman that fell off of the balcony?"

"Yes, of course we have. The police in the entire Keys are on high alert because of those cases," said Officer Baldwin in her usual antagonistic manner.

"Well, I'm the concierge at the Casa Bella, and one of the group members is staying at The Moorings right now. Lillian Dumas."

Officer Baldwin listened up. "And you think she might have cut your brake line?"

Kelly nodded. "I can't imagine anyone would do that, but she'd be a suspect if anyone was."

"Key West has her fingerprints. I know the colleagues there have been looking for her, because she checked out of the Casa Bella so suddenly and disappeared. We'll check the truck for fingerprints and compare them. I'm going to call Officer Sanchez in Key West and inform her about this. Do you have anyone who you can either stay with or who can give you a ride home? You'll need to come to the station with us and file a report. For your insurance too," she said, nodding at the truck.

Max is gonna be so mad about his truck, thought Kelly.

"How long will the truck have to stay with you guys?" she asked.

"It just takes our forensics department a few hours to check for fingerprints and take photos," replied Officer Baldwin. She looked at her watch. "It's four p.m. now, so they won't get much more done today, and we'll have to have it towed because of the brakes, of course. Let's say until tomorrow around noon?" She looked at Officer Pratt who nodded to confirm. "Do you have someone who can fix it tomorrow?" she asked Kelly.

"I hope so," Kelly, looking for Jose's business card in her wallet. "Jose Gomez in Islamorada."

Everyone knew everybody in the Keys. "Oh, yeah, he's a great guy," said Officer Pratt. "If you call him now, you might still catch him before he closes for the day."

"Can we take you back to The Moorings?" asked Officer Baldwin.

Kelly had no idea where to go and if she should stay over or go home, but Susan seemed like her first option. She nodded but also called Gilda to ask her for advice.

"Oh, my poor little chica!" Gilda exclaimed. "Boy, you've bad luck with that truck! If I didn't have to take care of the kitten, I'd come and get you!"

With all that was going on, Kelly had totally forgotten about Zoë and felt bad. And she did have to work tomorrow and had no change of clothes or toiletries with her.

"I am going to try and come down tonight because I need to work tomorrow, and who knows when the truck will eventually be released from forensics and fixed. I'm going to let you go, I need to call Jose now before he closes the shop."

Gilda replied, "Good luck. Let me think about how I can help. And don't worry about the kitten. I've got this. You can make it up to me when I have my orchid show on Saturday."

In the meantime, Officers Sanchez and Brinkmann jumped into their car and headed up to Islamorada. Simultaneously, they emailed Lillian Dumas' fingerprints to the police station in Marathon.

Officers Baldwin and Pratt and Kelly had arrived at The Moorings, walked up to the office, and asked for Lillian Dumas' room number.

"Oh, Ms. Dumas just left. She was down at the beach until half an hour ago with her friend because she had a late check out, but she left at four-thirty. I think she's headed to Miami now."

Officer Baldwin stomped her feet on the ground and had to restrain herself from throwing her phone onto the ground as well. Officer Pratt secretly snickered. He knew his boss's hot temper too well that tended to get her in trouble sometimes.

"Okay, she might be in Key Largo by now or almost in Homestead. Pratt, please inform our colleagues there. We're looking for a blonde in a red Mustang convertible."

Pratt nodded and called their colleagues in Key Largo and Homestead.

Officer Baldwin turned toward Susan. "May we have the key to Ms. Dumas' cottage? Maybe we'll find something useful there. I assume it hasn't been cleaned yet?"

"No. Nobody's checking into that cottage today, so we weren't going to clean it until tomorrow morning," replied Susan. She looked at a big wooden board on the wall with old-fashioned style keys hanging from it, grabbed on of them and handed it to Officer Baldwin. "I can lead you to the cottage," she said and walked around the front desk.

The two officers searched the messy cottage and found some scribbled down phone numbers, but they didn't seem to have anything to do with the case. Officer Baldwin put the notes into a forensics bag, just in case.

"I really wish we knew what we're looking for," muttered Officer Baldwin, "and I'd really like to know what Kelly Palmer has to do with these incidents…"

Suddenly, Officer Pratt, who was inspecting the bathroom, yelled, "Well, this is interesting! We're not looking for a blonde in a Mustang convertible anymore. We're looking for a brunette!" He held up a box of L'Oréal permanent hair color number six.

Chapter Thirty-One

"Well, that's interesting news," said Officer Baldwin. "She sure is a sneaky one, and she must be hiding something. Let's call everyone and let them know. She could be trying to get away from us or just from Ryan Goslan—or just have colored her hair for fun." She grinned. 'Hey, I need to color mine every four weeks. Pratt, can you please find out whether the truck has been towed yet? I really want to see if we can find some fingerprints."

Kelly was hanging out with Susan in her office. Susan offered to let Kelly take her car home if she needed to get back today. "I live so close, I can take my bike to work," she said. "And with Brent working from home we barely need his car."

"I might take you up on that offer, since that would work out perfectly, considering I need to come back and pick up the truck again. Tomorrow is my last day, so I really need to be there. And the tech group that's been so cursed is leaving tomorrow as well, believe it or not. I probably need to see them off with Charles…"

"Oh, no," said Susan. "I'm sure he's the last person in the world you want to see."

Kelly shuddered. "Yup. But it's the last time— unless I freelance for that hotel."

Little did Kelly know that Charles had already been accompanied out of the hotel by the owner and a security guard, carrying a box of his belongings, to never return to the Casa Bella. The entire management was being replaced due to the unfortunate series of VT Tech incidents. Even Kelly's position was eliminated. A full-time concierge was no longer required. She'd find out sooner than later.

Suddenly, there was a loud commotion outside that made Kelly and Susan look out of the window. The groundkeeper had obviously met someone he was happy to see. The two men were hugging each other and talking excitedly in Spanish. Kelly recognized Ricky! The groundkeeper was another one of his many uncles. It seemed half of Islamorada's population belonged to Gilda and Ricky's family.

Kelly ran out and asked, "What are you doing here, Ricky? You should already be halfway to Orlando!"

He walked up to her quickly. "Well, my mom called me and told me you had an accident, and I thought I'd turn around and check on you. I don't really have to be in Orlando until tomorrow. Are you okay? What happened?"

"It seems like someone cut the truck's brake line. It was fine after I left Jose's shop and must've happened when I stopped here." Kelly was so happy to see Ricky that she almost hugged him, but she restrained herself.

"Why would someone do that?" he asked. "Who would want to harm you?" He seemed very upset.

"Well, the police think it might have to do with the case that's been going on at the Casa Bella."

Ricky had heard about it from his mother. "But what do you have to do with that group?"

"I don't know. One of the members of that group was staying here now and might have seen me. I don't know why she would want to harm me though, except if she's heard your mom and me talking about the case." Suddenly Kelly had an epiphany. "Or she still thinks I told the police that she was here! I never thought about that!"

"Where is this woman now?" asked Ricky.

"You must have passed her. She seems to be on her way to Miami. The police are looking for her."

"I wish there was more I could do," said Ricky.

"Well..." replied Kelly. She knew what he could do. She really didn't feel like driving by herself after getting so shaken up with the failing brakes this afternoon. "I need to get back to Key West tonight. It's my last day tomorrow, and I really need to be there, but I don't feel like driving all the way back by myself after what happened. Wanna drive me?"

He smiled. "Of course! I'd love to. But only if I can take you out for dinner tonight. I already have a place in mind."

Kelly was tired after the long day, but that was the

least she could do after Ricky was wasting hours of driving around. And – she didn't mind his company at all. She smiled at him. "Well, I'm the one who should be taking you out." There was tension in the air as their eyes met, and they both smiled.

As Kelly and Ricky started driving back toward Key West, Kelly called Officer Baldwin first.

"Hi, Ms. Palmer. What can I do for you?"

"Hi, I just wanted to remind you that I called the police after I saw Ms. Dumas on the beach at The Moorings," said Kelly. "She might've heard me."

"Yes, we're aware of that, but—please keep this between you and me—Ms. Dumas' fingerprints don't match the ones on the truck. Although of course she might have hired someone to do it."

"Okay, thanks. I just wanted to make sure you were aware of her possibly being mad at me," said Kelly.

"Thank you," replied Officer Baldwin. "We're investigating in all directions. We're also trying to find out who the lady was who was with her today."

Kelly ended the call, and she and Ricky were silent for a while and enjoyed golden hour, the last hour before sunset when the sun was so low that everything was aglow and dipped in a golden light. They drove through Marathon and then onto the spectacular Seven Mile Bridge, the ocean on both sides glistening. Kelly closed her eyes. As they arrived on the south side of the bridge, Ricky turned into the parking lot, took her in his arms, and kissed her in the evening sun.

Suddenly, Kelly heard Latin jazz and startled. She was so comfortable that she had fallen asleep, and Ricky hadn't noticed.

"Oh, I'm sorry, I can turn the music back off," he apologized and turned the knob to turn the radio off.

"I'm sorry, I must've dozed off," she replied and smiled at him, realizing what she had just dreamed. She was a bit disappointed that the kiss had only happened in her dream. "Go ahead and turn the music back on. It was nice."

"Okay, and feel free to sleep a little more," he grinned, "the longer you nap now, the longer we can party tonight."

She looked at him, a little shocked. With the kitten and everything else going on, she wasn't sure how long she'd be able to stay out.

"I'm just kidding," he said. "I know you have a lot going on with your work, the broken truck, moving in with my mom and the kitten. We can even get takeout if you want."

She nodded. "That would be nice." And she fell back asleep.

Chapter Thirty-Two

Kelly snapped awake, just as Ricky exited the Overseas Highway and took a right onto Roosevelt Blvd. He was talking on the phone and didn't sound very amused. A female voice was very obviously reprimanding him in Spanish. He looked very uncomfortable and just threw in a "Yeah, yeah, yeah," from time to time. As soon as he saw out of the corner of his eye that Kelly was awake, he said briefly, "Gotta go," and ended the call.

"Sorry about that," he said as he nervously stroked through his thick dark hair. "I hope I didn't wake you up." He didn't go into detail about the phone call, even though his phone was heating up with the blinking with incoming text messages, and Kelly didn't either. If she guessed she would've thought that it sounded like he was being yelled at by an unhappy girlfriend because he wasn't coming home tonight.

"Oh, I'm okay," she said and smiled. "I'm sorry that I was such a boring passenger, but I'm exhausted from the last few days, and somehow this comfortable seat put me to sleep."

"It was lovely to watch you sleep. I'm glad you felt

so relaxed and comfortable," he replied.

She smiled again and blushed a little. She felt comfortable around him but didn't really want to admit it yet and now she was a bit nervous about the woman on the phone.

"By the way, my mom is making *arroz con pollo* tonight, so that's it for going out to dinner. But her *arroz con pollo* will be the best you've ever had."

Kelly didn't mind at all and had to secretly chuckle about what she'd heard about Cuban men and their mothers. They were brought up very spoiled and their mamás always came first. "That sounds delicious," she replied.

Since Lillian Dumas was so annoyed by her vacation being interrupted by the police dragging her back to Key West, she had extended it again and changed her plans. She exited the Turnpike in Fort Lauderdale, followed her GPS to the cruise ship terminal and pulled into the parking lot leading to the high-speed ferry to the Bahamas. She presented her passport, went through customs, and boarded the ferry. Her phone rang. She looked at the display. It showed that Ryan was calling. Without hesitating, she reached over the railing and dropped her phone into the water. Then, without further ado, she got a new one out of her purse and turned it on. She smiled at a good-looking middle-aged fellow passenger who looked like he was also traveling solo as she sat down next to him, her brown hair and her beautiful tropical caftan flowing in the gentle Atlantic breeze around her tall slender body. She and her fellow passenger were already in a lively and pleasant conversation as the ferry departed for the Bahamas and walked over to the bar to get themselves drinks. The police were checking all airports, but nobody had thought of this method of transportation or that she'd even leave the country. Officers Baldwin and Sanchez were fuming…

Ricky pulled the BMW into the driveway of his mom's house, and he and Kelly got out and walked into the house. Just as they entered the kitchen where loud Latin music was playing, a noisy alarm on Gilda's phone went off. She was wearing a nice flowery dress underneath an apron and was in the middle of stirring and chopping something at the same time. The kitchen smelled heavenly, with something delicious baking in the oven. Without even greeting them or turning the music down, Gilda turned the noisy alarm off and ordered, "Hey, you guys, you can take care of Zoë. It's time to feed her." She stopped in her tracks for a second, dropped everything she was doing and ran over to Kelly, almost starting to cry. "Let me give you a hug, *chica*.

I'm so glad you're okay! That must've been so scary!"

Then she hugged Ricky and gave him a big smooch on the cheek. "And you, thanks for getting her! Oh, I love you, *hijo mio*!" Kelly just stood there, perplexed, but Ricky was used to being bossed around and kissed by his kind-hearted mother, who was used to having everything under control.

He knew, if she said the kitten had to be fed, it had to be now, not in a few minutes.

"Ma, where's the kitten milk? Do we have to mix a new batch, or is there some in the fridge?"

"It's in the fridge. Microwave some water in a cup for forty-five seconds, and then warm the bottle up in there. But don't get in my way. I'm almost done with dinner."

Since Ricky was taking care of the kitten milk, Kelly knew her thankless task was to stimulate the kitten to pee again and headed sighing toward the bathroom. But Gilda yelled, "Oh, Kelly, she's peeing on her own now!"

So, Kelly just went to wash her hands and get the kitten out of the crate. Zoë had grown since the last time Kelly had seen her and was getting very feisty. By the time Kelly had opened the crate's door, the kitten had already climbed halfway up the metal grid and hung there, clamoring for attention, and demanding to get out.

Ricky took over the feeding, and Kelly enjoyed watching how gentle and loving he handled the little kitten, even though she was feisty and tried to chew up the nipple several times. Even after they were done feeding Zoë, which was routine now, they sat on the bathroom floor with crossed legs, playing with her as she climbed from Ricky to Kelly and almost fell, trying to crawl into her shirt.

Ricky caught the kitten and brushed Kelly's arm which felt almost like an electrical shock. They both felt the tension. Ricky looked through his thick long eyelashes into her eyes, but Kelly was nervous and looked down at the kitten. Kelly knew she was falling for him, but first she needed to find out who the woman on the phone was.

Gilda, who took her apron off and hung it on a hook on the back of a door, called from the kitchen. "Dinner's ready!" A deliciously steaming meal of arroz con pollo, in a giant cast-iron pan, was waiting for them on the kitchen table. The table was set like for a special occasion and looked like Gilda had gotten out her best china. A beautiful tropical flower arrangement, that Gilda had made herself, served as the centerpiece.

"Help yourselves," said Gilda and Kelly realized how hungry she was. Suddenly, Gilda's phone beeped with an incoming message. Then another one. It seemed urgent. Gilda apologized and checked her phone. *Can you please tell Ricky to call me back? He's not returning my calls and messages. Sofia.*

"Nothing urgent," she said and continued eating her dinner.

Chapter Thirty-Three

After dinner and a delicious caramel flan dessert that had Kelly swooning and wanting more, she offered to do the dishes. She started clearing the table, while Gilda wanted to go and check on the kitten one more time. Ricky started helping Kelly, but Gilda gave him a side look.

"Ricky, can you please help me in the bedroom for a second? I need you to help me lift a heavy box into the closet…"

"Sure," he said unsuspectingly. He set the stack of dishes down next to the sink that he had collected from the table, smiled briefly at Kelly, and followed his mother down the hallway.

"What's going on between you and Sofia?" Gilda hissed at Ricky as soon as she thought Kelly was out of earshot. "I thought you guys broke up! Why is she texting me?"

"What'ya mean, she's texting you?" he asked, alarmed.

"She just texted me during dinner to tell you to call her because you aren't returning her calls. Don't get yourself into trouble again, son. Clear things with one girl before you start something with the next. I can see how you're flirting with Kelly. Don't hurt her. She's a good friend of mine."

"Mom," he replied, a bit too loud, so that Kelly became aware that they were arguing and started paying attention, even though she tried not to. "It's not my fault. Sofia is a psycho. She won't accept the fact that we broke up weeks ago. She's even badmouthing me on social media…"

Kelly didn't want to eavesdrop and purposely turned the faucet on to start rinsing off plates and putting them into the dishwasher. She also turned on some quiet music on her phone. She had already heard too much and wanted to cry that Ricky obviously had so much baggage. Did she only fall in love with married men or men coming out of troublesome relationships?

A few minutes later, Ricky and Gilda returned to the kitchen and helped Kelly do the remainder of the dishes although she had worked so furiously that she was almost done.

"Wow are you participating in some sort of dish marathon?" asked Ricky grinning, as he stepped up to her and smoothly took a plate from her hands that she was drying. Their hands touched coincidently, and they both almost backed up, feeling the electricity between them. Ricky looked at her through his thick eyelashes while Kelly tried to avoid eye contact.

"Kelly, I'm having another glass of wine on the porch. Would you like to join me?" asked Gilda. Kelly looked at the big wall clock above the kitchen door. It was 8:30 pm. Tomorrow was her last day, and she was tired from all the driving back and forth, but it was still a bit early to go to bed, so she nodded. "Sure. Thanks." They both walked out onto the front porch while Ricky went up to his room.

"So, what did the police say about your 'accident?' Did they think it's related to the case?" asked Gilda, trying to change the subject to something neutral and not to be too curious about Kelly's feelings for Ricky.

"I think the woman who was staying at The Moorings, Lillian Dumas, might have heard me tell the police that she was there. So, she is the main suspect, but her fingerprints are nowhere on the truck."

"Well, she wouldn't have done that herself. She would have hired someone. I wouldn't know how to cut a brake line, would you?"

Kelly shook her head. "She left just about ten minutes before the police got there to talk to her, and now they can't trace her again. She is either super lucky or knows how to hide from the police. She keeps getting away from them."

"And how about the murder and the other cases? Any news?"

"No, I as far as I know, they just keep going from Ryan Goslan to Lillian and back. And Ryan seems to be just sitting around, drinking all day, since Lillian is gone. That doesn't make him seem very guilty. And thank goodness Max was found innocent and had an alibi as well. That was a bit scary."

"I wonder if this will be a case that's never solved," said Gilda, rolling her eyes. She took a sip of wine and went on to more pleasant things. "So, what are you doing this weekend? I'm organizing a big orchid show at the Key West Garden Club at the West Martello Tower. You need to come!"

"After tomorrow, I'll have nothing going on. I'd love to come, even though I'll be broke and without income and won't be able to buy many orchids."

"Oh, you'll be fine. And, hey, you just help some vendors with their stands, and they'll give you free orchids. You'll land on your feet. I'm going to introduce you to my friend Maria, who also freelances as a concierge. Maybe you can even help her with some of her clients in the beginning. She's super busy. You can also help me with the plant business, if all else fails."

"Thanks, Gilda. You've been a lifesaver with everything."

They sat on the cozy porch overlooking the overgrown front yard, listening to the Key West nighttime noises. A screech owl hooted, some frogs in a little pond croaked, and a foghorn tooted somewhere in the distance. A sudden wind came up. The bamboo canes clunking together produced a gentle, hollow knocking sound that Kelly found very calming. Gilda, who knew what the sudden wind meant, pulled the little table and some cushions away from the wooden railing, and she was right. Seconds later, heavy raindrops came splattering down, and the typical daily rain poured down, getting the sides of the porch wet. The first thunderclap made Kelly jump, but then she sat there with her new friend and enjoyed the lightning show from her safe, covered location. The spectacle lasted only about ten minutes, and then it was over but had brought much needed cooler temperatures. Kelly and Gilda felt like they could breathe again after it had been hot and humid all day.

"It feels nice, doesn't it?" asked Gilda and Kelly nodded. She emptied her glass of wine and said, "Well, I'm going to bed. I'm beat. Today was a long day, and I need to be in good shape tomorrow."

"Okay. Yeah, that was a tough day. Good night, my dear, sweet dreams," said Gilda.

"Good night, and thanks for the wonderful dinner."

"My pleasure."

Kelly grabbed her empty wine glass and carried it over to the kitchen as Gilda poured herself another glass and grabbed her phone to check her emails. She still had a lot to organize for the orchid show this weekend. Right at that instance, Gilda's alarm went off again. It was time to feed the kitten. Every three hours. Kelly heard it, knew what it meant and offered, "I can do the feeding, Gilda."

"No, you go to bed. You can take over after tomorrow when you're not working anymore."

Kelly hesitated. She felt bad, but she did feel exhausted and needed some sleep.

"Okay, deal," she replied. "Good night!"

"Night." Gilda smiled, took another big sip of wine, and got up to feed the kitten.

Just as Kelly was walking up the tight staircase, Ricky came down. Kelly felt the butterflies in her stomach fluttering around again as she saw him.

"Oh, I wanted to have a glass of wine with you guys. Are you sure you're already going to bed? Just one glass?"

"Sorry, I'm really beat, and I have my last day of work tomorrow."

"Puhleeeeease?" He laughed, then changed his tone. "It's okay, I understand. I'm leaving tomorrow morning, so if I don't see you tomorrow, I wanted to say, I—I had fun driving with you today."

It was so cute of him to say that. She wanted to just melt away, take him in her arms, and kiss him, but her shyness and the thought of the possible girlfriend or even ex-girlfriend scared her a little. So, she just said, "Yeah, I had fun too. I guess I'll see you this weekend?"

"Yeah, I'll be back Friday. Good night." He couldn't help himself and had to give her a quick peck on the cheek, but then he turned around quickly without turning around again. Kelly stood there for a second, watching him leave, but then she also turned around and walked up the stairs. She realized again that it was a bit awkward that they had to share a bathroom, but she hurried up, took a quick shower, and brushed her teeth while she heard Ricky talking to his mom on the porch. She made sure that there were no traces of herself in the bathroom and retreated into her room quickly, making sure Ricky didn't see her in her cozy yet not very sexy plaid bathrobe and slippers. Kelly was exhausted, the bed was comfortable, and the sheets smelled freshly washed, but she tossed and turned, listening to Ricky's and Gilda's muffled voices, and couldn't sleep.

A while later, she heard Ricky coming upstairs, trying to be quiet, but of course she was concentrating on him and could hear every single sound he made and every single creaking wooden floorboard as he tiptoed down the hallway. They both tossed and turned until the early morning hours and wanted nothing more than to be brave enough to slip into the other one's room and start kissing each other, but they didn't. Finally, as the roosters had already started crowing, they were graced with a few hours of sleep.

Chapter Thirty-Four

K elly startled as her alarm went off at seven a.m. She had barely slept for three hours and wasn't very rested. She quickly turned the alarm off, and her first thought was Ricky again. She hoped she hadn't woken him up since the walls here seemed paper thin. She heard his bed creaking on the other side of the hallway, and the butterflies in her stomach started fluttering again. She waited for a second to avoid running into him on her way to the bathroom, but he was quiet. He had obviously just turned around or fallen back asleep again. She grabbed her bag with her toiletries, threw her bathrobe on, rushed into the bathroom, and locked the door.

As she stepped out of the bathroom and walked down the hallway with a towel wrapped around her head, she could hear Gilda clanging around downstairs in the kitchen. To her horror, Ricky's door opened, and he staggered out, still half asleep, wearing only a pair of boxer shorts with his hair sticking up in all directions! He seemed embarrassed himself for a second, but then he grinned and looked at her through his long, thick eyelashes as he apologized. "Oh, hey there. I'm sorry, I forgot I have a roommate now."

He looked extremely hot, even now or especially now, but she wondered if he knew it. She just whispered, "Morning," and disappeared quickly into her room, her heart racing. This was too much for her this early in the morning!

Gilda had already made scrambled eggs with bacon, toast, and coffee. Ricky was already sitting at the breakfast table shoveling large amounts of food into his mouth, as Kelly stepped into the kitchen and sat down.

"Hey, Sunshine," Gilda said smiling and poured Kelly a cup of coffee. "Milk and sugar are right here if you need them." She pointed at a little set of cream and sugar dispensers on the table. "Eggs, bacon, and toast?"

Kelly nodded and Gilda turned around and made her a plate. Kelly had no time to continue being nervous around Ricky, because, half a minute later, he jumped up.

"Bye, Kelly. Bye Mom. I've got to go. I have rehearsal with Professor Randall at three, so I'm cutting it close with the seven-hour drive. Wish me luck."

He smiled at Kelly and gave his mother a big smooch on the cheek. She quickly wrapped her arms around him and wouldn't let go of him. He laughed and yelled, "Maaa! I really need to go!"

"Bye, Chiqui. Drive careful. Love you."

"Love ya," he replied and stormed out of the house. They could hear his BMW drive up the gravel driveway and turn onto the street. Gilda sighed. "I hate when he drives all the way up to Orlando with so little time. At least he got a good night's sleep, I guess."

Kelly didn't reply but wondered if he had. She had heard him tossing and turning all night on his squeaky mattress, just like her.

Today was not only Kelly's last day of work at the Casa Bella, but also the VT Tech group's day of departure after their five-day-stay at the resort. Officers Sanchez and Brinkmann were upset that they had to leave today and wouldn't be available for them at their beck and call anymore, but there was nothing more they could do to hold them. Kelly was surprised when she got off her bike, walked over to the dock to wait for the ferry, and ran into Officers Sanchez and Brinkmann, who were also waiting, pacing, and looking at their watches. That meant something must've happened again.

"Good morning, officers. I know it's none of my business, but may I ask if something happened again? Otherwise, you wouldn't be on your way to the Casa Bella again this early, would you?"

The officers recognized and greeted her with

serious faces. Bianca replied, "Good morning, Kelly. Yeah, we're not supposed to talk about it, but you'll find out in five minutes anyhow: Max, the head chef, fell down the old fire ladder leading up to the secret rooftop terrace. We don't know if it was an accident or if he was pushed."

"Celine, his sous chef, said he's not doing very well," added Officer Brinkmann. "We think he's been lying there all night, and he seems to have at least a bad concussion."

Two chickens darted out of the way as an ambulance pulled up. Two paramedics climbed out and grabbed a stretcher and a case full of medical supplies. They greeted and joined them as they all climbed onto the ferry that had just arrived.

Kelly was horrified. Her friend Max. She hoped he wasn't seriously injured and felt bad that she hadn't been there for him more the past few days after he had been so kind to lend her his truck. And why him? Now the theory that someone wanted to get rid of his or her competition didn't work anymore because Max certainly wasn't competition at VT Tech anymore. Kelly asked, "You guys know that Max also used to work for VT Tech, don't you?" "Yes, we figured that out when we questioned him after the last incident. Thanks," snapped Bianca, a bit insulted. She was starting to feel like her abilities as an investigator were being questioned. They really couldn't afford to not solve this case.

The ferry arrived at Little Orchid Island's welcome

station, and everyone climbed onto the dock. Celine, Max's second in command in the kitchen, was already waiting and led the way to the fire ladder on the side of the building next to the kitchen entrance. "Where's Charles?" asked Kelly, wondering why Celine was doing this and not Charles.

Celine looked at her, surprised. "You don't know that he was fired?"

Kelly was flabbergasted. "No, I had no idea!"

There was no time to go into detail about that because they had reached Max, who was lying on the ground. He had quite a deep laceration on his head and had been placed in the lateral recumbent position with a shirt under his head and covered with a blanket. Another kitchen staff member had been sitting next to him, holding a clean towel to the wound on his head. Max was conscious but quiet. He seemed to be in shock. Kelly and the two police officers stayed back so that the paramedics could do their job, but Max recognized her and started stammering. "Kelly, Kelly…i-it was a g-ghost, and she pushed me!"

Kelly and the two officers looked at each other, their eyebrows raised.

The head paramedic kneeled next to Max and got a small flashlight out of his kit. He asked, "Sir, can you hear me?"

Max nodded.

"What's your name?"

"Max Freeman."

"Can you please follow this light with your eyes?" And he shone the light from left to right, checking

Max's pupils and reflexes.

"I think he has a concussion, but we'll definitely have to do an MRI at the hospital to rule out any skull fractures or other complications," said the paramedic. "That wound needs a few stitches, but it's not too deep. Head wounds always look terrible because of the excessive bleeding."

"Does anything else hurt, Mr. Freeman? Can you move your arms and legs?"

Max wiggled his arms and legs and nodded. But then he twitched because his head hurt.

"Kelly, G-Gilda's right about the ghost," he stammered again, trying to make eye contact with Kelly. Kelly came closer, kneeled next to Max, and took his hand. "Okay, the police officers are right here. They'll take care of it. Do you want me to go to the hospital with you?" He nodded. Then he was lifted onto the stretcher, and the paramedics got ready to carry him toward the ferry.

"How long do you think it will take until we can question him?" asked Bianca.

"We'll have to do the MRI and wait for the results, but probably just a few hours. Thankfully, he's fully conscious and has no amnesia. Looks like he had a guardian angel. Who knows from which height he fell," replied the paramedic, looking up at the rusty ladder.

"Well, I can tell you right now," replied Bianca, who was looking up at the ladder with her sharp eyes as well and had spied something. She put on a pair of rubber gloves, climbed up the ladder, and at about ten feet, she pulled her phone out of her pocket with one hand and took a photo. Then she pulled an approximately three-inch by three-inch piece of white gauze out of a notch in the rusty metal step, nudging it back and forth a little. She turned around, looked down at the group on the ground, and asked, "What would you say? About ten feet? I'm wondering if Max tried to follow her and then fell as he tried to hold on to her by her dress."

Max closed his eyes and nodded slightly.

The paramedics made their way back to the dock, followed by Kelly. There was so much she had to find out and take care of, but this was more important right now.

Chapter Thirty-Five

Kelly waited in the hallway of Lower Keys Medical Center while Max was having his MRI. Now that she had almost lost her friend, the worst thoughts raced through her mind. She suddenly appreciated all the things she had taken for granted before. She knew that he had more than friendly feelings for her that she didn't share, though she enjoyed knowing that someone liked her and thought she was attractive. Had she been taking advantage of him? She felt awful. She had used his car every time she needed it, she had poured her heart out to him about Charles when she knew it probably hurt him, he had boosted her ego, and she hadn't done anything for him in return.

As Max was wheeled into his appointed room in his bed, she followed him, smiled, and sat next to his bed.

"Any results yet?" Kelly asked the nurse.

In this instance, a doctor walked into the room. "You were very lucky, Mr. Freeman. It looks like you have no serious injuries. You only have a bad concussion, and we'd like to keep you here for a couple of nights."

"We gave him some pain medication, so he might sleep for quite a while now," the nurse said to Kelly.

Max looked briefly at her and said groggily, "I've always had a head of steel, ha-ha. Thanks, Kelly, for being here."

"Of course, Max. I'll get you a few things from home if you'd like. Just let me know what you need."

Max was already asleep. *I guess the rule that you're not allowed to sleep with a concussion doesn't count if you're in a hospital,* thought Kelly. She looked at the time on her phone. It was 9:30 a.m. She'd have a few hours to go back to the Casa Bella now, talk to the kitchen staff and Officers Brinkmann and Sanchez and find out what might have happened to Max. And Charles! She wondered what had happened. Then she'd take care of the VT Tech group departing at eleven, pack her things and say some last goodbyes before she went over to Max's condo and got him some T-shirts, underwear, pajamas, and a toothbrush. After that, she really had to go and pick up Max's truck, but that didn't seem urgent anymore. She also had to get up to the police station in Marathon and sign her statement…

Meanwhile, at the Casa Bella, Officer Bianca Sanchez was reprimanding Officer Stone who was on the island to keep an eye on things. Once again, he had obviously been hanging out with Ken Miller and Ryan Goslan, rather than doing his rounds and paying attention to what was happening.

"Where were you?" she snapped at him. "Drinking with Ryan Goslan and Ken Miller again?"

It was frustrating that, despite this island being so confined and having a sergeant on location to keep an eye on things, something like this could happen. The perpetrator must still be there....

"Go check the fire ladder, the rooftop terrace and all the surroundings one more time and see if you find anything. More parts of the gown. Other evidence. Footprints. I shouldn't have to tell you."

Embarrassed, Officer Stone stepped away and started searching the ground around the fire ladder. He climbed up the fire ladder, which was quite dangerous in and of itself, and started looking around there. He got a bit distracted by the beautiful view from up there and wanted to sit down and take a break when he suddenly discovered something. The door leading inside was slightly ajar, and there was a pink hair ribbon on the ground. Without moving the possibly very important piece of evidence, he called Officers Brinkmann and Sanchez who were still below him, near the side kitchen entrance. "Michael, Bianca! I found something. Wanna come up and see, or shall I bag it?"

Bianca's head shot up. "Don't touch it! We'll be right up!"

Instead of climbing up the treacherous fire ladder,

they ran inside the kitchen to a door. Behind the door was a steep wooden staircase leading upstairs to the rooftop terrace. They walked carefully, still checking the area for other evidence but were soon upstairs and saw the pink ribbon as well. Bianca put on her rubber gloves and gave herself the honor of picking it up and putting it in a plastic bag after examining it a bit more. It said Lilly Pulitzer all over it, in small letters. "Well, the perpetrator seems to be a woman." She looked at Brinkmann and stated, "The remaining women in the group are not here, so it's an outsider. And it wasn't a ghost." Then she looked at Officer Stone. who was proud that he had found something and made up for not paying attention and preventing the new incident (which was basically impossible anyway since the property was quite large). "Good job, Officer Stone."

Kelly had just returned from the hospital and walked straight to the side kitchen entrance to see if Officers Sanchez and Brinkmann were still there and had any news. They had just come back down and were stepping out of the kitchen entrance. "Oh, hi, Kelly. How is Max doing? We were just on our way to the hospital to question him about the incident," said Bianca.

"He's not as bad as he looked at first. He was very lucky. No broken bones and no internal injuries or damage to his head. Just the laceration and a bad concussion."

"Well, that's good news. I'm curious how he got the laceration falling backwards down a ladder," Bianca said, almost to herself.

Kelly spotted the bag with the Lilly Pulitzer ribbon that Bianca was still holding in her hand.

"May I?" she asked as she took a closer look. "I've seen that somewhere before," she said, also lost in her thoughts.

"What? The ribbon?" Bianca's attention was immediately riveted on Kelly. "Why don't you guys keep searching the grounds for other evidence and footprints, and I'll go to the lobby with Kelly," she said to her two colleagues. "I want to talk to the front desk personnel too."

As Bianca and Kelly walked around the building toward the back pool entrance, Bianca asked again, holding the bag with the ribbon up, "So, any ideas where you might've seen this before?"

"I just remember that a guest was wearing it, but I can't remember who it was," Kelly replied. So much had happened in the past few days that it was all a blur. "Just give me a few minutes. I'll remember," she said with a smile. Bianca didn't want to give her a few minutes but had no other choice.

As soon as the two women stepped into the lobby, Ken Miller rolled up in his wheelchair. "Officer Sanchez, my colleague Ryan Goslan and I have come to the conclusion that we know Max Freeman. He used to work at VT Tech!"

"We are already aware of that, but thanks for your input, Mr. Miller."

"So, the sixth VT Tech victim so far! Have you questioned the remaining six colleagues? It must be one of them."

"Yes, Mr. Miller, and thanks," she said, rolling her eyes. "We've been working around the clock. Trust me, we've investigated in every direction so far."

"Okay, just a thought..." He realized that she was annoyed and rolled back over to his friend Ryan, who was sitting at the bar in the restaurant having what didn't seem to be his first Bloody Mary with his late breakfast or early lunch.

"Everyone wants to be a sleuth in this matter," Bianca sighed and turned back toward Kelly who was now sitting behind her desk. "Mr. Miller and Mr. Goslan keep calling me with ideas they think might be important, as well as about eight other VT Tech employees and other hotel guests..."

Kelly could see her frustration and wished she could help her. She looked at the ribbon again and tried to remember where she had seen it before. In this instance, Gilda stepped into the lobby, her arms full of fresh flowers. Another distraction, thought Kelly, even though she was happy to see Gilda. Gilda walked straight up to Kelly and Bianca.

"Buenas dias, ladies," she said. "I just saw that strange lady at the ferry. Remember the 'entitled' one you told me about, Kelly? Who was so upset when the pool couldn't be used on the day Samantha Berg died? The one that's always wearing pink Lilly Pulitzer outfits?"

Bianca and Kelly looked at each other with big eyes.

"That's her," Kelly said breathlessly. "A lady who's been asking me a lot of questions about the VT

Tech group too. She always seemed strangely curious. She's staying in the Palm Suite." She paused for a second, but then she remembered. "Marilyn McGaffy!"

"I wouldn't be so sure she's staying in the Palm Suite anymore. I think she had at least a carry-on suitcase with her. She might've checked out," said Gilda.

Kelly, followed by Bianca, got up and ran over to the front desk, where Claire was checking in some new guests.

"I'm really sorry to interrupt," said Kelly, "but this is an emergency!"

"What kind of customer service is this?" asked the guest, taken aback, while shaking his head.

"We are so sorry," interrupted Bianca, "but this is regarding an ongoing police investigation. It's urgent. I'm sure the hotel can make it up to you somehow." She looked at Claire who nodded, got out some breakfast vouchers and showed them to the guest. He seemed to be pleased, nodded at his wife, and stepped aside.

"Claire, we need to know if Marilyn McGaffy checked out today. Or is she still in the Palm Suite?" asked Kelly.

"Just a second." Claire typed something and stared at her screen. "Sorry, she checked out about half an hour ago."

Bianca looked at Kelly and moaned. She couldn't believe her bad luck. And the ferry with Ms. McGaffy had obviously also already left when Gilda arrived about ten minutes ago. So, the next one wasn't coming for another twenty minutes. She called her colleagues at the Key West Police Department, explained the situation, and a search warrant for Marilyn McGaffy was issued immediately.

Kelly walked back to her desk and googled Marilyn McGaffy. Nothing came up under Marilyn, but there were lots of articles and photos under Lisa McGaffy, who had been one of the most successful employees at VT Tech for the past three years until she suffered a nervous breakdown and burnout syndrome a few months earlier. She was now obviously in a mental institution. Lisa McGaffy was Marilyn McGaffy's daughter!

Chapter Thirty-Six

Bianca called Officer Brinkmann, and they rushed over to catch the next ferry to the mainland. Several police cars had been dispatched to the intersection of Overseas Highway and Roosevelt Boulevard and to the airport, but Marilyn McGaffy seemed to have vanished into thin air. Since there was only one road out of Key West or the alternative of flying, and Marilyn McGaffy very well knew that the police might be searching for her, she could still be hiding somewhere in Key West. The ferry personnel hadn't paid attention to where she went, nor had she taken the resort's airport shuttle.

Bianca was beside herself with anger that, just like Lillian Dumas, Marilyn McGaffy had gotten away.

"Dammit," she yelled, then she took a few breaths to calm down. She looked at Michael and asked him, "Any ideas?"

He shook his head. They just stood there like beaten dogs, knowing their boss wouldn't be too happy about the new development. "All we can do is put a search warrant out, inform the public, and wait and see if we get any leads," said Michael. Bianca nodded. "Let's go to the hospital and talk to Freeman."

Meanwhile, Kelly had been called into Charles' former office, where the owners were taking care of things on an interim basis with their human resources manager Andrew, a young man in a dark blue suit and a white button up shirt. He was sweating and his face was red. There had been a lot of layoffs. The employees were nervous, and he was stressed out.

"Please take a seat, Ms. Palmer," said Mr. Lourdes, who was standing next to the desk where his wife, a beautiful tall brunette in her late forties, was sitting in Charles' chair. "As you probably heard, we had to let our current management go. It was more a political move, since the string of unfortunate events with the VT Tech group has been casting dark shadows on the resort's reputation," he explained in flowery language. "To save money and since this has always been a family business, we are going to run the hotel ourselves for a while with our daughter Sandy who's currently flying in from New York. You worked with Sandy when she trained at the front desk and might remember her. We value you as an employee, but we're sorry to inform you that we find we currently don't currently require a fulltime concierge. It's come to our attention though that you are planning on freelancing in the same capacity, and we'd like to offer you the opportunity to stay parttime on a temporary basis until we've figured things out. Sandy will be living in the main house with us, but unfortunately, we're going to need the guesthouse apartment for her assistant, who's coming along as well."

Kelly processed the information. It was nothing surprising for a company to switch employees from full-time to part-time or to temporary contracts to save on paying health insurance and other benefits. Since she had planned on leaving anyhow, it was quite nice to have at least a parttime job to pay some bills until she knew what she was doing as a freelancer and had established her own clientele. She smiled and nodded. Her reason for leaving, Charles, was gone now and she had always liked the Lourdes and their daughter Sandy. "Thank you, I'd love to continue working for you."

"Okay, then Andrew and you can go to his office and discuss your new agreement. We'd also like to thank you for your help in finding the perpetrator of the crimes that were committed here. It's still not one hundred percent confirmed that it was Mrs. McGaffy, but we heard that you and Ms. Gomez were a big asset for the police in connecting her to the crimes." He looked at his watch. "It's ten-thirty. Will you be available at eleven a.m. to see off the VT Tech group as a familiar face for them?"

Kelly looked at Andrew, who nodded. She said, "Sure. And thank you very much."

At 11:00 a.m., Kelly and Andrew were done setting up her new contract, which she was very happy with. She had fewer benefits, but her hourly rate was much higher than it had been before, so she would be able to slowly ease into freelancing and keep up a certain standard of living.

Kelly rushed into the lobby, where the members of VT Tech were already gathering with their designer suitcases. This time, it was only eight men; the two women were missing. One dead, one missing in action. The bellboys lifted the luggage onto rolling carts, and they all headed toward the ferry station. Ryan Goslan pushed his friend Ken Miller in the wheelchair. The atmosphere was subdued after everyone had found out that Lisa McGaffy's mother had possibly committed the crimes. Lisa had been a very competitive, successful, and attractive colleague. Most of the men were guilty of hitting on her to the point of sexual harassment just because of her position in the company, even though she had made it very clear that she was not interested in any of them after having failed relationships with Max and Ryan Goslan. Some of them couldn't blame her mother for wanting to get revenge for how her daughter had been treated. Most of them stated they weren't aware that Lisa had several breakdowns and was now in a mental institution, although some of the incidents had happened at work and many had witnessed them.

"Well, have a safe trip home, everyone," said Kelly. Even though she knew it was bad for the police, she was relieved that the group was finally leaving. "The shuttle to the airport is waiting for you at the dock. We hope you enjoyed your stay at the Casa Bella despite all the issues." She looked at Ken. "I've arranged for you to have special assistance at the airport, Mr. Miller. Enjoy your flight home." He nodded and said, "Thank you for everything." He switched over to a pair of crutches as Ryan Goslan folded his wheelchair. Two other colleagues helped him onto the ferry. Mr. and Mrs. Lourdes who had already spoken with and shaken everyone's hands in the lobby, were now standing in the background, waving, and saying one last goodbye. Then Mrs. Lourdes said quietly, "Well done, Kelly." They all sighed in relief that this chapter was now over.

Kelly, who now didn't officially have her last day anymore, went back to her desk for a while and had the farewell cake the front desk colleagues had brought for her, which was now a welcome cake. Then she took the next ferry to go and see Max in the hospital. As she walked in, Officers Sanchez and Brinkmann were just leaving Max's room, again with no new information. Max had talked about a ghost again and seemed to be hallucinating as far as Bianca and Michael were concerned.

To Kelly's surprise Celine, Max's sous chef, was

sitting next to Max's bed, holding his hand. As soon as Kelly stepped into the room, Celine blushed and quickly pulled her hand away, but Kelly had seen enough to be happy for Max. She hoped he'd find love with Celine and remain her good friend.

Kelly stepped up and held up the duffel bag full of clothes and toiletries. "Hey, Celine. Great to see you. I brought a few things, Max. How are you feeling?"

He tried to sit up, but the pain in his head made him cringe and remain in his current position. Celine instinctively reached out and put her hand on his shoulder to hold him back. Kelly could tell that she had strong feelings for him and was upset about his injury.

"I'm okay," he said with a weak voice.

"Have they found out yet why you have that wound on your forehead?"

"I think the person—or the ghost—hit me with something. Maybe a rock. That's why I fell backwards in the first place." He closed his eyes, and Kelly looked at Celine with a quizzical expression. Celine shrugged. She didn't know if Max was hallucinating or not. Who was she to say that ghosts didn't exist, and wasn't there a rumor that the hotel was haunted? Although it did sound crazy.

"Max, they found a piece of gauze from a gown and a Lilly Pulitzer ribbon on the rooftop terrace. Do you remember Lisa McGaffy?"

He nodded. He had dated her for a while when he still worked for VT Tech. "What does she have to do with anything?" he asked upset.

Kelly realized she might be getting him upset and regretted saying something, but it was too late now.

"Her mom has been staying at the hotel and was constantly wearing Lilly Pulitzer clothes and that ribbon as well."

Max became even paler than he was. He closed his eyes and shifted toward the wall.

"Well, I'm sorry I mentioned this," said Kelly. "Max, I'll be at the apartment packing up more stuff to take over to Gilda's. Let me know if you need anything else. Is it okay with you if your truck stays up in Islamorada for one or two more days? I guess you don't need it right now and I don't know who could drive me up there today."

Max had barely heard her. He was still upset thinking about Lisa McGaffy. He had been a witness to her nervous breakdown, and her leaving the company had caused a big commotion since she had been so close to being number one a few times. He nodded slightly. He didn't care about the truck right now.

"Maybe I can drive you," Celine offered quietly as she walked Kelly out to the hallway.

"Thanks," replied Kelly. "Boy, I wish I hadn't said anything about Lisa and Marilyn McGaffy. That seemed to really upset him."

"The police officers who were here right before you said the same thing. It really upset him. I guess they were engaged at some point..."

"Oh boy, poor Max," said Kelly. "This must have brought back some bad memories. Maybe that's why in his subconscious he'd prefer it was a ghost."

As Kelly left the hospital, a few local journalists and photographers approached her. "Hi, you work at the Casa Bella, don't you? Aren't you the concierge? Do you think the head chef Max Freeman was attacked by a ghost, or has the perpetrator finally been identified? Or are the police still grasping in the dark?" Oh, boy, thought Kelly. She decided not to answer and just kept walking quickly. Things were getting a bit too crazy in her opinion, and she'd probably get in trouble for saying anything...

Chapter Thirty-Seven

T hree days later, Kelly was all moved into Gilda's house. The series of unfortunate events at the Casa Bella seemed almost forgotten, except that Officers Sanchez and Brinkmann were still desperately searching for Marilyn McGaffy and Lillian Dumas and not having much luck. Kelly was taking a bit of time off from work and getting into the swing of things, helping more with the kitten, while Gilda was super busy preparing for her orchid society's big show on Saturday.

Zoë was making giant steps. She had started eating some solid food and was getting so playful that Gilda was considering getting another kitten in her age, so that she had a playmate. She was feisty, wanted entertainment, and didn't want to stay in her crate anymore.

Gilda was in the kitchen making breakfast again as Kelly stepped in to get a cup of coffee. "Good morning, beautiful! How about some breakfast? I just made some eggs."

"Sure, thanks, but Gilda, you need to stop feeding me these giant meals every morning or I'm not going to fit into my clothes pretty soon."

"Oh, come on. At your age you can eat as much as you want." Gilda laughed.

"No, I can't. Look how tight these pants are already getting in my waist," replied Kelly, tugging at two inches of skin that she considered fat.

Gilda laughed. "That's not fat. Wait until you're my age. It accumulates just by looking at food." She changed the subject. "But enough of that, I've got to hurry. I'm meeting some volunteers and vendors for the orchid show at the Garden Club, and we're going to finish setting up the displays today. I think we're quite shorthanded, so I'm a bit stressed."

Kelly swallowed her last bite of eggs, jumped up, and took some dishes over to the sink. "Gilda, seriously, I can help. I wouldn't really know what I'm doing, but I'm a body, and I'd love to learn. I just fed Zoë, so I have a window of opportunity right now. And she's been sleeping longer, and the gaps between the feedings are getting bigger."

"I'd love that. We could really use the help. We have smaller displays than other orchid shows but more since we have a lot of small rooms in the fort that we need to decorate. We also need to provide the vendors from abroad with tables and supplies that they couldn't bring with them, so it's a lot of hauling stuff around."

Kelly nodded. She was game for everything.

Gilda continued, "Also, what's a lot of fun, the vendors had to ship the orchids they're going to be selling to themselves and need to unpack them. It's like Christmas, even though the presents are not for us." She grinned. "You can imagine that the orchids from Brazil are even more exciting than our local ones."

Kelly had no idea what Gilda was talking about. Her orchid knowledge was limited to Phaleonopses from Publix or Trader Joe's, and she was proud she even knew that name.

Even though the Garden Club at the West Martello Tower was not further than a ten- minute walk, they took Gilda's old Volvo station wagon. She had too many plants and orchids that she was taking with her. They were already sitting in the driveway in front of the house, all cleaned up and ready to be exhibited at the orchid show. Gilda opened a hidden garage door on the side of the house that Kelly hadn't even noticed yet. She started the old car that wasn't taken out very much. It sputtered a few times, but then its reliable Volvo motor finally worked, and the car slowly chugged out of the small one-car garage and up the driveway with Gilda behind the steering wheel. They quickly opened the back hatch, loaded the orchids inside, and drove over to the West Martello Tower, past the Casa Marina and Clarence S. Higgs Memorial Beach, on the south side of Key West. The car backfired and sputtered and was quite a sight because it was bright pink. People stopped and looked, as Gilda and Kelly drove by, surrounded by tropical plants.

People were already rustling and bustling at the Key West Garden Club at West Martello Tower. They greeted Gilda and immediately helped unload the car and carry the orchids inside the old fort, built with red bricks during the Civil War. Kelly, who was introduced and welcomed by everyone in a very friendly manner, was ashamed that she had never been here and, more importantly, that she had never recommended this beautiful destination to her guests. It was a spacious old fort sprawling along the beach with cavernous rooms, brick walkways, outlooks, and little nooks everywhere. The members of the Garden Club seemed to be decorating every inch with tropical plants and orchids. Kelly hauled orchids inside or to the exterior areas and helped hang them onto shepherd's hooks and stands or lifted them onto displays. The shady interior with the thick brick walls was nice and cool for shade-loving plants, while the outside walkways and walls housed cacti, tropical vines, plumerias, palm trees, and other plants that could withstand the relentless sun of the sub-tropics.

Kelly worked hard and the time passed quickly. Gilda, who had been looking for her, walked up and said, "Wow, you're doing a great job, Kelly! Thanks so much for helping."

Kelly smiled. She had really enjoyed working with the plants and was amazed about how much she had learned today and how many new friends she had made. It was such a nice change from sitting behind her desk every day, although she knew that her whole body would be aching from the unusual exercise tomorrow.

"Don't forget about Ricky's concert tonight. Are

you still planning on going?"

Kelly hadn't forgotten because Ricky was always in her thoughts and they had even texted back and forth a bit earlier, but she was shocked to find out how late it already was. The concert was starting in about an hour.

"We should get going and have something to eat and start getting ready."

"Yes, I can't believe how I lost track of time," replied Kelly. "This was so much fun!"

One of the Brazilian vendors, a man in his sixties with a giant mustache and a thick unibrow, came up to Kelly and handed her a gorgeous blooming Cattleya with dark-red and pink spotted petals.

"*Obrigado* for your help today," he said in his strong Brazilian accent. "I couldn't have done it without you. If you want, help me with my stand tomorrow, and I'll have more orchids for you."

Gilda admired the beautiful orchid. "See, I told you so." She grinned. "Your orchid collection will be as big as mine in no time."

Chapter Thirty-Eight

Kelly and Gilda rushed up busy Duval Street, dodging tourists partying on the sidewalks, following the sound of Ricky's tenor saxophone that they could already hear from afar. Obviously, they were late, and the band had already started playing. They quickly squeezed through the audience, made their way to the stage, and got there just as the first song was ending with one of Ricky's solos.

Gilda yelled "Bravo!" as the audience started clapping. Ricky made eye contact with both his mother and Kelly, hinted a bow, and smiled. He was obviously pleased to see that Kelly was there, and her heart fluttered in her chest as she looked into those dark soulful eyes with the thick eyelashes. She was wearing a flowery pheasant dress in green tones that matched her green eyes and brunette hair and sandals that were stylish yet comfortable enough to dance in for hours, and she felt very good about herself. *Tonight's the night,* she thought. She was going to go for it and try to have some alone time with Ricky after the concert and not be as shy as usual.

Just like last time, the band played funky Latin jazz that put the crowd in a good mood and made them want to dance. Gilda and Kelly put their arms in the air and danced to the music. Suddenly someone stepped up to Gilda and tapped her on the shoulder. Gilda turned around and froze. Ricky, on stage, who had just looked at Gilda and Kelly again, almost stopped playing, he was so upset when he saw who it was. It was Sofia, his ex- girlfriend.

Gilda greeted her and introduced Kelly. She had always gotten along well with Sofia and didn't want to get in the middle. "Buenas tardes, Sofia, this is my friend Kelly." Kelly and Sofia nodded at each other. "What brings you all the way down to Key West?" "I'm visiting my friend Ana and thought I'd come and see Ricky too." "Ana, this is Ricky's mom Gilda and her friend Kelly." Another pretty girl stepped up and said hi to everyone, and they all started speaking Spanish. Kelly with a few years of school Spanish under her belt was lost in translation very soon and couldn't follow the conversation. She listened to the music but now had a moment to take a closer look at Sofia. She looked like a model. She was 5'10" tall, had peach blonde hair, beautiful skin, a perfectly shaped face and beautiful eyes and lips, and Kelly found her very intimidating. What did Ricky find in her? She wasn't unattractive, but she certainly wasn't a super model like this girl. Sofia did look like she had worked quite hard on her perfect appearance though.

They all clapped as the band ended the next song. Gilda stepped up to Kelly. "I'm so sorry that we all started speaking Spanish. That was quite rude."

"That's okay. I was glad that I could concentrate on the music and didn't have to chit chat," she replied and grinned.

As soon as the concert was over and Ricky came out from behind the stage, Sofia was all over him and trying to flirt. For a moment, Kelly's heart slipped into her pants, and she wanted to leave. But Ricky wasn't interested in Sofia's advances, stepped over to Kelly and let everyone know that she was his date tonight by putting his arm around her as he thanked the group for coming. Gilda took some pictures of Ricky and Kelly, and Kelly took some of Ricky and Gilda. Sofia and her friend stuck around for a while but then finally realized that Ricky wasn't interested and left with another group that was going clubbing. Gilda nudged Ricky in the side as they left. "She'll get over it," said Ricky. "Look how she's already flirting with that guy." Gilda nodded and said quietly to Ricky, "Well, that was a shock when she showed up. I didn't think she'd leave without a fight." Kelly heard what Gilda said but decided not to let Sofia ruin her evening and didn't pay attention. She was happy right now and nothing else mattered.

"I need to go home and get some sleep, kids," said Gilda who also knew that Ricky and Kelly needed some privacy. "The orchid show starts at 9 a.m. and I need to be there at 8 and start cooking egg sandwiches at 7. We're serving breakfast for the vendors."

Kelly felt obliged to go home with her and wanted to help in the morning as well, but Ricky looked at her with his big brown eyes and pleaded, "Just one drink?"

"Sure," she said and smiled. She needed a drink to calm her nerves down. Her heart was out of control again.

The concert crowd thinned out as everyone was going their way, either to a late meal or to the next concert or party. Friday evenings in Key West were very busy, and often the partying didn't stop until the early morning. Ricky said goodbye to his band mates, grabbed his saxophone in its case, and he, Gilda and Kelly started heading back toward mid-town. It was a beautiful balmy evening, and they walked down the busy street past bars and cafes with music and laughter coming out of the entrances. Gilda had to take a left, and Ricky said, "Ma, we're going to keep going to Manuel's bar at the end of Duval."

"Okay, kids, have fun," she said and smiled.

"Manuel's" was a little bar at the end of Duval right on the ocean, rather romantic and different than the bars they were passing right now, full of noisy heavily drinking people.

Kelly and Ricky kept walking straight. They were leaving the party mile behind and entering a quieter area. They walked past the Key West Butterfly and Nature Conservatory, the Southernmost House and right behind that was "Manuel's", a little porch on a dock with just a bar, the name in neon letters and a few little tables scattered about. Manuel himself was standing behind the bar, pouring some vodka into a cocktail glass in a professional manner by lifting the bottle higher and higher. Just about four other people were sitting at the tables and the bar. Manuel recognized Ricky and shouted out in excitement, "Hey, amigo! Sorry I couldn't make it to your concert! How was it?"

"It was fun! Next time. I know you're working."

"Manuel, this is my friend Kelly," Ricky introduced.

Manuel nodded and said, "Hi, Kelly," as he examined her. He liked what he saw. A real woman and not like that fake super model. He had never been fond of Sofia. "What can I get you?"

"Hi, Manuel, nice to meet you. Can I please have a Cosmo with Tito's?"

"I'll have a beer," said Ricky.

Some other guests came up. Ricky and Kelly grabbed their drinks and walked over to one of the tables. The moon was full and bright in the clear sky, and its reflections were sparkling in the water. It was balmy and humid but felt good with a slight breeze so close to the water.

They toasted and had a sip of their drinks. They both looked silently into the dark water, but then Ricky put his hand on Kelly's and said, "I'm sorry that you had to deal with my ex. She's been quite a pain. We broke up four weeks ago and, even though she was the one who wanted to break up, she's changed her mind for some reason." He paused and looked into Kelly's eyes. "But I haven't."

Their eyes locked and they were about to kiss, when a noisy group of people came walking up the dock. It was Sofia and her new friends who were quite rowdy in the meantime.

Chapter Thirty-Nine

Manuel was highly alarmed when he recognized Sofia, and so was Ricky. The group stepped up to the bar and started placing their orders, but the area was so small that they were also intruding on Ricky and Kelly's space. Sofia smiled at Ricky, asked, "May I?" and sat down without waiting for an answer. "It's so great to see you again," she said and put her hand on Ricky's.

Kelly witnessed Ricky's hot temper for the first time. He pulled his hand away from under Sofia's, hissed, "Leave us alone," at her and said to Kelly, "Let's go." Kelly didn't hesitate, got up and quickly walked down the dock without turning around. Unfortunately, Ricky wasn't as fast as her. One of the men in the group, a rather musclebound guy, with giant abs and tight sleeves, stopped him and said, "Hey, man, I think you should apologize to Sofia for talking to her like that."

"Ricky scoffed and replied short, "I don't think so, man."

Before Ricky could even think twice, the guy had punched him in the face so hard that he almost fell backwards off the dock. Ricky was able to catch himself and was about to hit back, when the other men in the group all pulled their friend along and quickly left the premises. Ricky was in so much pain that he had to sit down again, holding his nose.

Alarmed, Kelly ran back down the dock, kneeled next to his chair, and asked anxiously, "Ricky, are you okay?"

Manuel came up with a towel and a bag of ice and carefully put it on Ricky's nose. "Do you think it's broken? We might have to get you to the hospital."

"Just give me a few minutes," Ricky mumbled a bit benumbed. "I think I'm okay."

Kelly looked at Manuel, horrified. He whispered, "He'll be okay." He had seen worse.

A few minutes later Ricky took the icepack off his nose and said, "I think I'm okay. Nice first date, huh?"

He grinned, but Kelly couldn't quite find his words funny, pulled up her nose and her eyes filled up with tears.

She took him in her arms crying – and they finally kissed.

The next morning, Kelly startled up from her sleep when her alarm went off at 7:00 a.m. She quickly hit the snooze button and realized that Ricky was lying next to her, snoring a little. She snuck out of the room, picking up some underwear on her way, as quietly as she could. Ricky only moaned briefly, turned around in his bed and continued snoring.

Kelly took a quick shower and got ready for the

day as she thought about last night. What had seemed like an unpleasant ending to a great night when Ricky got punched by his ex's friend, had finally gotten Ricky and Kelly together. She had felt so sorry for him that she had to take him in her arms, and one thing lead to the next. She blushed a little, thinking about last night, but she was happy and very much in love. She hated the fact that she was tied up all day, but maybe Ricky would come and visit at the orchid show.

Gilda was already carrying several trays covered with aluminum foil to her car, she had been up for a couple of hours, preparing countless breakfast sandwiches and breakfast burritos for the orchid society members and vendors. Kelly prepared the kitten milk and went to the back of the house and took care of Zoë who wasn't too happy when Kelly left again. She needs a playmate, thought Kelly. She made a note to text and remind Ricky that he had to feed and maybe play with her in a few hours.

"What a beautiful day," said Gilda, as she and Kelly drove the short drive to the Garden Club in Gilda's old Volvo. It had rained during the night, everything looked fresh and luscious, and it wasn't as hot as usual. "You look like you're glowing," Gilda said to Kelly. "Are things going well between you and Ricky?" Kelly blushed. She hoped Gilda hadn't heard anything, but all she said was, "Yes, we had a great evening." She wasn't sure how things were going to work out living in her 'mother-in-law's' house and was a bit nervous about that detail. She didn't mention Ricky getting punched, he should decide himself whether he wanted to tell his mom or not.

Gilda parked the car in one of the employee parking spaces, and they both grabbed the food trays from the back and carried them inside.

The Garden Club was rustling and bustling with activity. Everyone was taking care of some last-minute things to get ready for the show. Some people were still finishing up the displays, two cashiers at the entrance were counting the money in their money boxes, the vendors were still adding orchids to their overflowing sales tables. Gilda and Kelly set down the trays on a table next to two big coffee percolators and some cut fruit, and everyone came up and grabbed a breakfast sandwich or burrito.

"Obrigado, I was starving," said the Portuguese orchid vendor and smiled at Kelly, then he recognized her. "Oh, Kelly, are you going to help me with my stand today? I could use another set of hands."

"I'm not sure what Gilda wants me to do, but I'm sure I can help for a few hours," replied Kelly. She wanted to help but didn't want to get stuck all day either, because she also hoped to have some time off and enjoy the show.

Soon it was 9 a.m., and an endless stream of people started arriving. They paid the entrance fee of $5 which went to the orchid society and walked from stand to stand, enjoying the beautiful orchids and other tropical plants like hoyas and philodendrons. Kelly looked for the Brazilian vendor's stand and assisted him with sales and did quite a good job. She was amazed about how much people paid for a single orchid. Some bigger plants were as much as $200, and people didn't blink twice paying that much if it was on their wish list. The endless stream of people never stopped until around noon, and the rooms of the Garden Club were almost too small for the crowds. Both Gilda, who was working at the entrance and stamping people who had paid admission, and Kelly didn't have a break until the early afternoon. Finally, they were able to take a break at the same time and walked around the exterior grounds where the guests thinned out a little but there were still some pretty displays and stands. Gilda pointed out some unusually colorful ginger plants to Kelly, and then she suddenly froze and stopped talking in mid-sentence. Kelly looked at her. Gilda wasn't usually startled that easily. Gilda pointed into a little room in front of them, which might have previously been a little office or even a cell, where two ladies were admiring some orchids. Gilda whispered, "That's Marilyn McGaffy and Lillian Dumas. I swear." Kelly froze, flabbergasted. Gilda was right. She recognized them too. Finally, the two ladies were done admiring the display, turned around to leave the little room and recognized Gilda and Kelly from the hotel. They tried to squeeze past them, but Gilda acted spontaneously and PUSHED Marilyn McGaffy backwards into her friend Lillian Dumas. Then she pushed the heavy wooden door shut, assisted by Kelly, and turned the key in the lock! Marilyn McGaffy had finally gotten a taste of her own poison. Both women started yelling loudly and pounding against the door. "Let us out! Let us out! You can't just lock us up like this!"

"Call the police!" yelled Gilda under her breath. Kelly nervously fumbled her phone out of her pocket and called Officer Sanchez whose mobile phone she still had in her contacts. Seconds seemed to take forever, and Kelly had never been more thankful when Officer Sanchez finally picked up her phone. "Make sure they don't get out," said Officer Sanchez breathlessly. "We'll be there in less than five minutes." Countless people from the show came up to see what the commotion was and helped Gilda and Kelly hold the door closed. It seemed that the two trapped women were throwing themselves so desperately against the door that the old hinges or the old lock could break or even the door itself. Marilyn McGaffy and Lillian Dumas finally realized the big crowd outside and how ridiculously they were behaving. They had to accept the fact that they weren't going to be able to escape and just stood there, defeated, with hanging heads.

Chapter Forty

Officers Sanchez and Brinkmann in one police car, accompanied by two other police cars and four more officers, drove up to the fort with flashing lights, jumped out and asked the ladies at the entrance for directions. The other officers waited in front of the Garden Club, standing by, in case they were needed. Bianca and Michael ran through the first building, out into the first courtyard, through the next building and then into the back open-air area, where a whole crowd was now standing in front of one of the former prison cells. The crowd parted for them in the middle, and Bianca and Michael made their way toward the room that Marilyn McGaffy and Lillian Dumas had been locked into.

As they opened the old one hundred and fifty-year-old door, it basically fell apart from being mistreated in the last ten minutes. Marilyn McGaffy and Lillian Dumas, who had given up totally discouraged, were sitting on two nice chairs that belonged to the display. They got up and let the officers handcuff them and lead them away.

Officer Sanchez, who was now in the best of

moods and whose boss would be happy with her and Officer Brinkmann, patted Gilda's shoulder in a jovial manner. "You did it again. Great job, Gilda. And you too, Kelly."

"Please come into the station for a statement whenever you get a chance, but we'd appreciate if you could do it in the next couple of hours," requested Officer Brinkmann. "We can't wait to hear what happened and need to finish up the report for the chief as soon as possible."

Gilda and Kelly high-fived and then hugged each other. They still couldn't believe what had just happened.

At this moment, Ricky arrived. He had been sent to the back after asking for his mom and being recognized by most members of the orchid society. He stepped up to Kelly and Gilda with a smug grin on his face and gave them both a kiss, struggling to hide something behind his back.

"Guess what I just found in front of the building, totally abandoned?" The surprise meowed pitifully. Ricky pulled it out from behind his back and presented a dirty, approximately two- to three-month-old striped tabby kitten to Gilda and Kelly. She was almost the same age as Zoë and was going to make a perfect playmate for her.

"Her name is Leia. I think she looks like Princess Leia from Star Wars, and she's a fighter."

Everyone clapped as he handed the kitten to Gilda and took Kelly in his arms and kissed her.

Chapter Forty-One/Epilogue

A little while later, Kelly and Gilda drove over to the police station, which was just down the road near the airport, to make their statements and sign them. Officer Sanchez was in a jovial manner after being praised by the chief and explained the various incidents that had happened to the VT Tech group to Kelly and Gilda.

"So, ladies, most of the incidents have been clarified now." She rattled them down.

"During the first incident at the pool bar, Ms. Dumas pretended to be pushed so that she wouldn't be accused of helping Marilyn McGaffy in the following cases. Sneaky thing..."

"Yeah, she's a pretty good actress," interrupted Kelly. "I saw her right after falling into the pool, and she seemed really upset."

Bianca continued, "Samantha Berg's death the next day was supposedly an accident: Marilyn McGaffy was arguing with her, they had a scuffle, Ms. McGaffy pushed her, and she fell backwards off the balcony. Lillian Dumas helped Ms. McGaffy get the keys to the room from Ryan Goslan who had them lying around in his room and whose room was right between Ms. Dumas and Ms. Berg's, and Ms. Dumas also switched out Ms. Berg's antidepressants with placebos.

In the Ken Miller case, Marilyn McGaffy dressed up as the famous ghost, the famous author's mistress, and pushed Ken Miller down the stairs. He had dated and cheated on Lisa McGaffy with Samantha Berg, which was one of the reasons for her breakdown.

Nobody ever pushed Ryan Goslan off the boat. It was an accident, and he said he was pushed, because he was obviously embarrassed and didn't want to look unathletic or clumsy. He admitted lying about it to Lillian Dumas.

The dive boat incident with Lillian Dumas was obviously really an accident, since Lillian Dumas certainly wasn't suicidal or Marilyn McGaffy didn't want to harm her, so that's a liability of the dive company.

Conor Mitchum was pushed (unsuccessfully) by Marilyn McGaffy, again dressed up as a ghost."

Bianca looked at Kelly. "When you saw Lillian Dumas on the beach in Islamorada and a second person with her, that was Marilyn McGaffy. Her fingerprints revealed that she was the one who cut your brake hose."

"Wow!" Kelly became pale, remembering how helpless she had felt when her car wouldn't stop because the brakes weren't functioning.

"And finally, Marilyn McGaffy also hit Max with a rock when he was following her up the fire ladder and caused him to fall.

Lillian Dumas knew about all incidents and helped Marilyn McGaffy hide and keep her presence on the down low. She was Lisa McGaffy's best friend and had also been treated poorly by Ken Miller and some of the other colleagues. Ryan Goslan had been flirting with Samantha Berg, and she was afraid he'd leave her again."

They all looked at each other, relieved that the case had been solved. "What I can't fathom, is that Marilyn McGaffy was there the entire time, and nobody saw or recognized her," said Kelly.

"Shows you how people don't pay attention to others when they're that self-absorbed and entitled, and maybe most people really didn't know a former coworker's mom," said Bianca.

They all nodded. That was the truth.

As soon as Gilda and Kelly were back at the orchid show, one of Gilda's friends from the orchid society came running up. "Jane's giant specimen Cattleya amethystoglossa and some other really nice specimen plants from the display were stolen while everybody was paying attention to the two ladies being arrested!" Gilda's jaw dropped as she looked at Kelly. "Some of those are irreplaceable..."

Don't miss Kelly Palmer's next adventure in this series of tropical cozy mysteries, "The Missing Orchids" and find out if our friends are able to find the irreplaceable Cattleyas and how things continue with Kelly and Ricky! Sign up for my newsletter @ Birgittvanwormer.com or follow me on Facebook, Birgitt Van Wormer – writer, to find out when it's available!

Dear Reader

I hope you enjoyed my first cozy mystery. I love writing about my favorite places in the world, the Florida Keys and Key West being one of them, and I hope I was able to transport you to that very special place where chickens run through the streets, the smell of tropical flowers wafts through the air and you can hear the ocean and Caribbean steel drum music or Reggae almost everywhere. You get out of your car or plane, and you're immediately immersed in a tropical vacation atmosphere. Imagine working here in a hotel! It can be tough to be on duty while others are on vacation, but it's also a great privilege to be in this beautiful place every day and there's always lunch, time off after work and the weekend! Kelly has a very fun job, helping other people make the best of their vacation – I hope you enjoy following her day to day!

If you liked this book, please leave a review on Amazon, and please sign up for my monthly newsletter on my website

Birgittvanwormer.com
or Biggivanwormer.com

for updates on my latest books and other information. I really appreciate YOU! Thank you!

Acknowledgements

Last but not least, I thank my husband and two sons for always supporting me, my mother-in-law Lucille for being my biggest cheerleader and my friend Jane for always being there for me, proofreading and bouncing ideas back and forth.

Most importantly, thank you to the real Concierge Girl, Kelly Hopkins in Key West, who was the inspiration for this series.

Made in the USA
Columbia, SC
10 July 2023